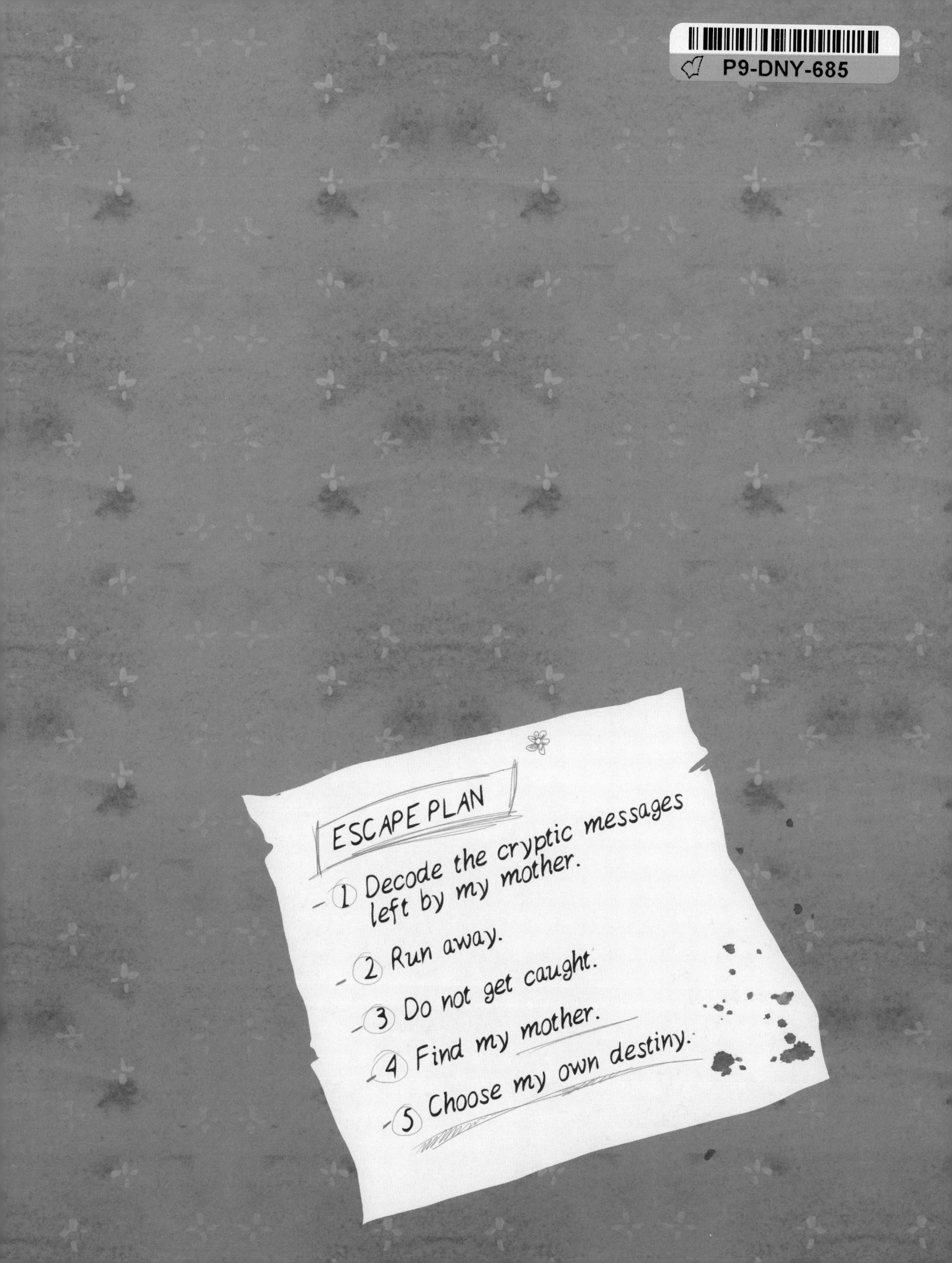
ESCAPE PLAN
1 Decode the cryptic messages left by my mother.
2 Run away.
3 Do not get caught.
4 Find my mother.
5 Choose my own destiny.

Serena Blasco

An Enola HOLMES Mystery

3. The Case of the Bizarre Bouquets

Based on the novel by Nancy Springer

EURO COMICS
ENGLISH EDITION   GRAPHIC NOVELS

An imprint of IDW Publishing

EuroComics.us

Editor Dean Mullaney
Art Director Lorraine Turner
Translation Jeremy Melloul
and Dean Mullaney

EuroComics is an imprint of IDW Publishing
a Division of Idea and Design Works, LLC
2765 Truxtun Road • San Diego, CA 92106
www.idwpublishing.com • EuroComics.us

IDW Publishing
Chris Ryall, President & Publisher/CCO
Cara Morrison, Chief Financial Officer • Matthew Ruzicka, Chief Accounting Officer
David Hedgecock, Associate Publisher • John Barber, Editor-in-Chief
Justin Eisinger, Editorial Director, Graphic Novels and Collections
Jerry Bennington, VP of New Product Development
Lorelei Bunjes, VP of Technology & Information Services • Jud Meyers, Sales Director
Anna Morrow, Marketing Director • Tara McCrillis, Director of Design & Production
Mike Ford, Director of Operations • Rebekah Cahalin, General Manager

Ted Adams and Robbie Robbins, IDW Founders

ISBN: 978-1-68405-642-2
First Printing, February 2020

Distributed to the book trade by Penguin Random House
Distributed to the comic book trade by Diamond Book Distributors

Based on the novel *The Case of the Bizarre Bouquets*
— *An Enola Holmes Mystery* by Nancy Springer
copyright © 2008 by Nancy Springer

Graphic adaptation copyright © 2016 Jungle, by Serena Blasco
originally published in France as *Le mystère des pavots blanc*

Special thanks to Flora Boffy-Prache of Steinkis Groupe, Justin Eisinger, and Alonzo Simon.

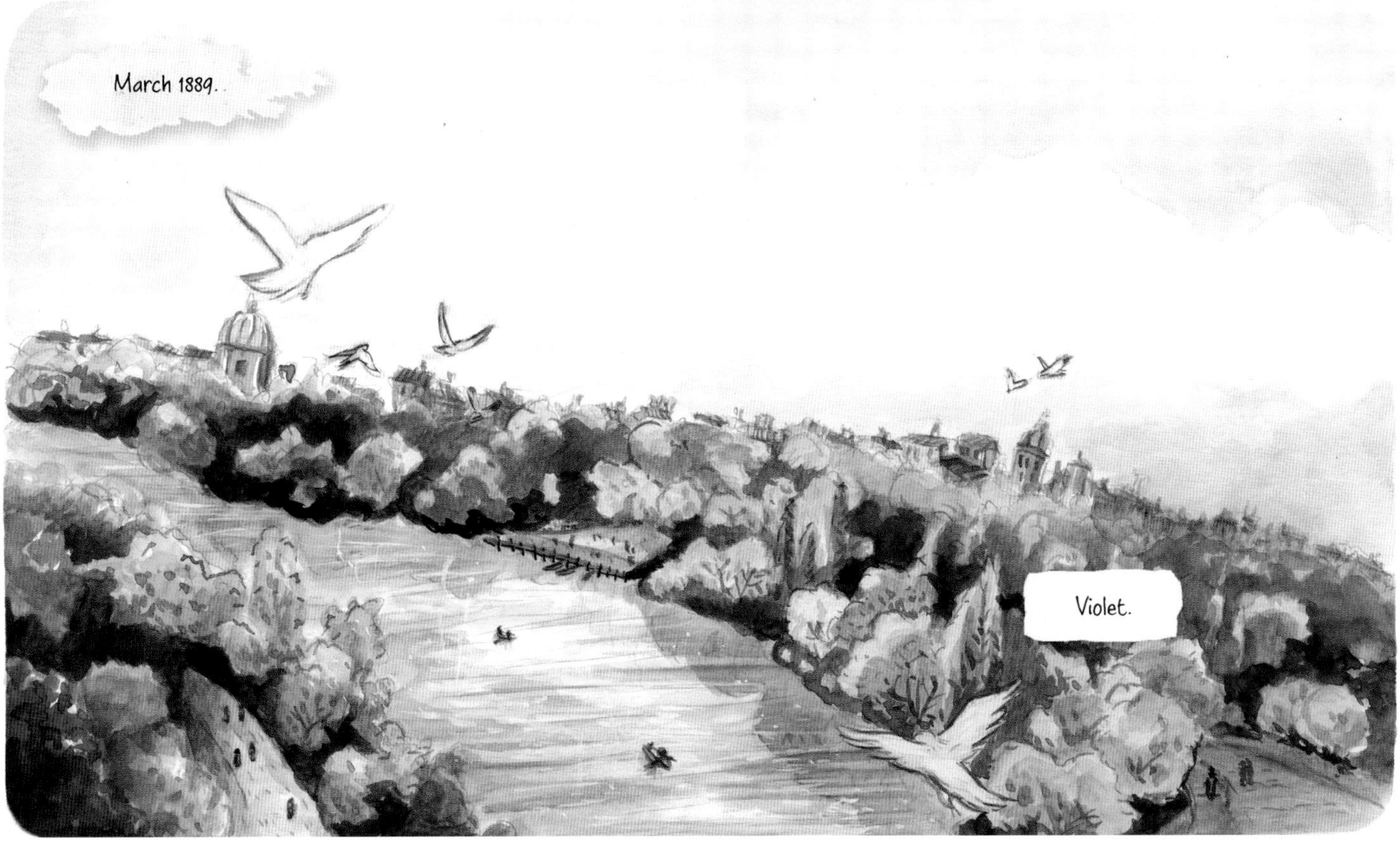
March 1889.
Violet.

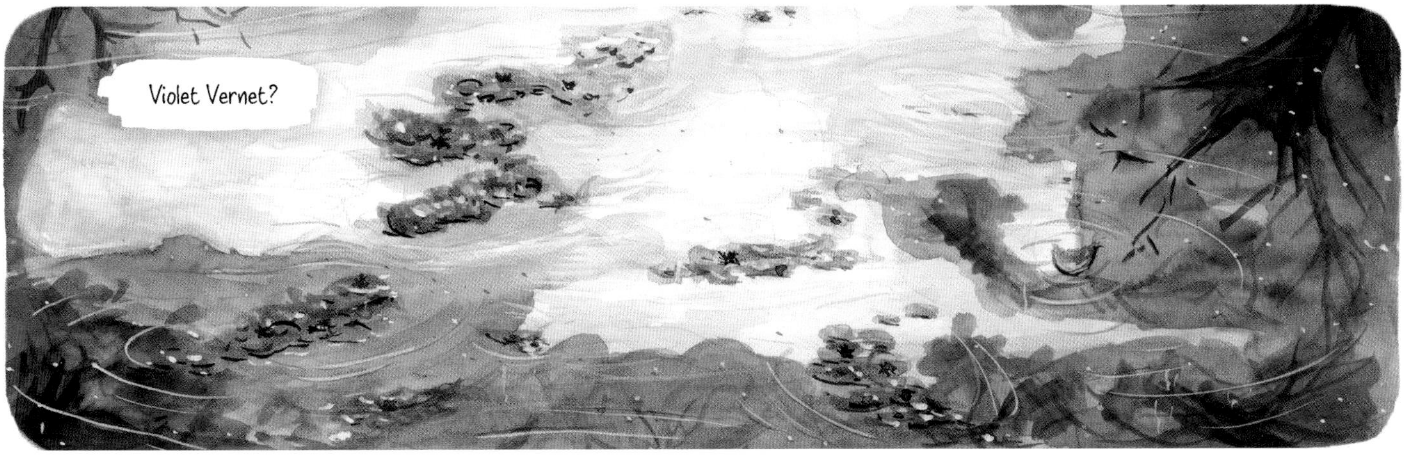
Violet Vernet?

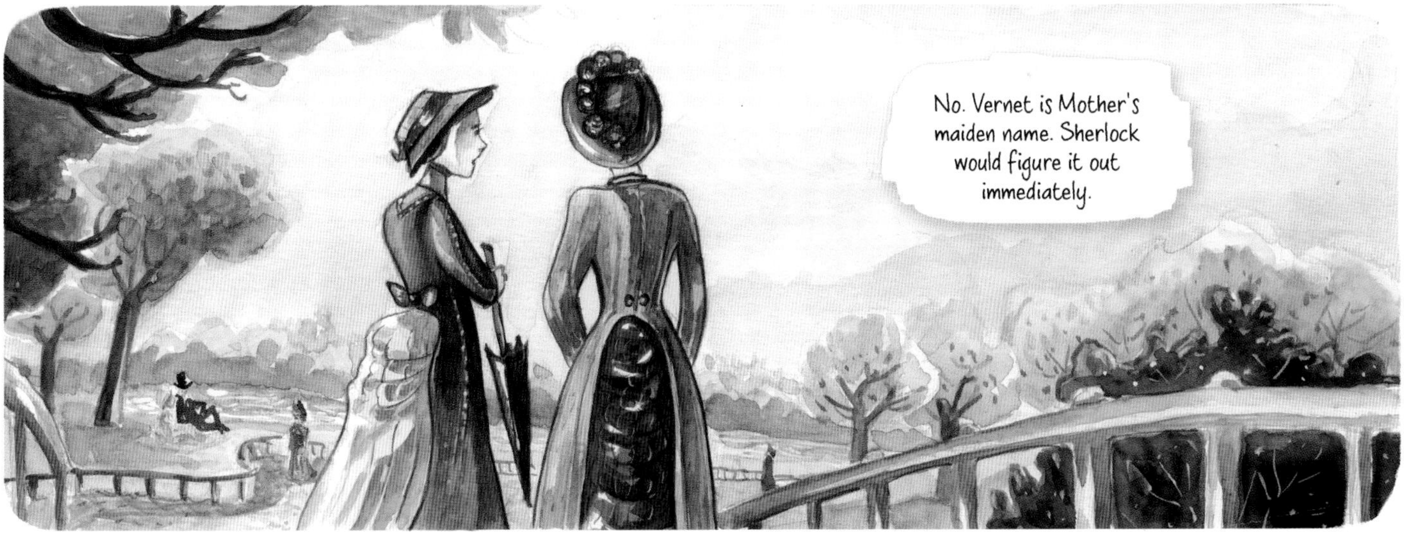
No. Vernet is Mother's maiden name. Sherlock would figure it out immediately.

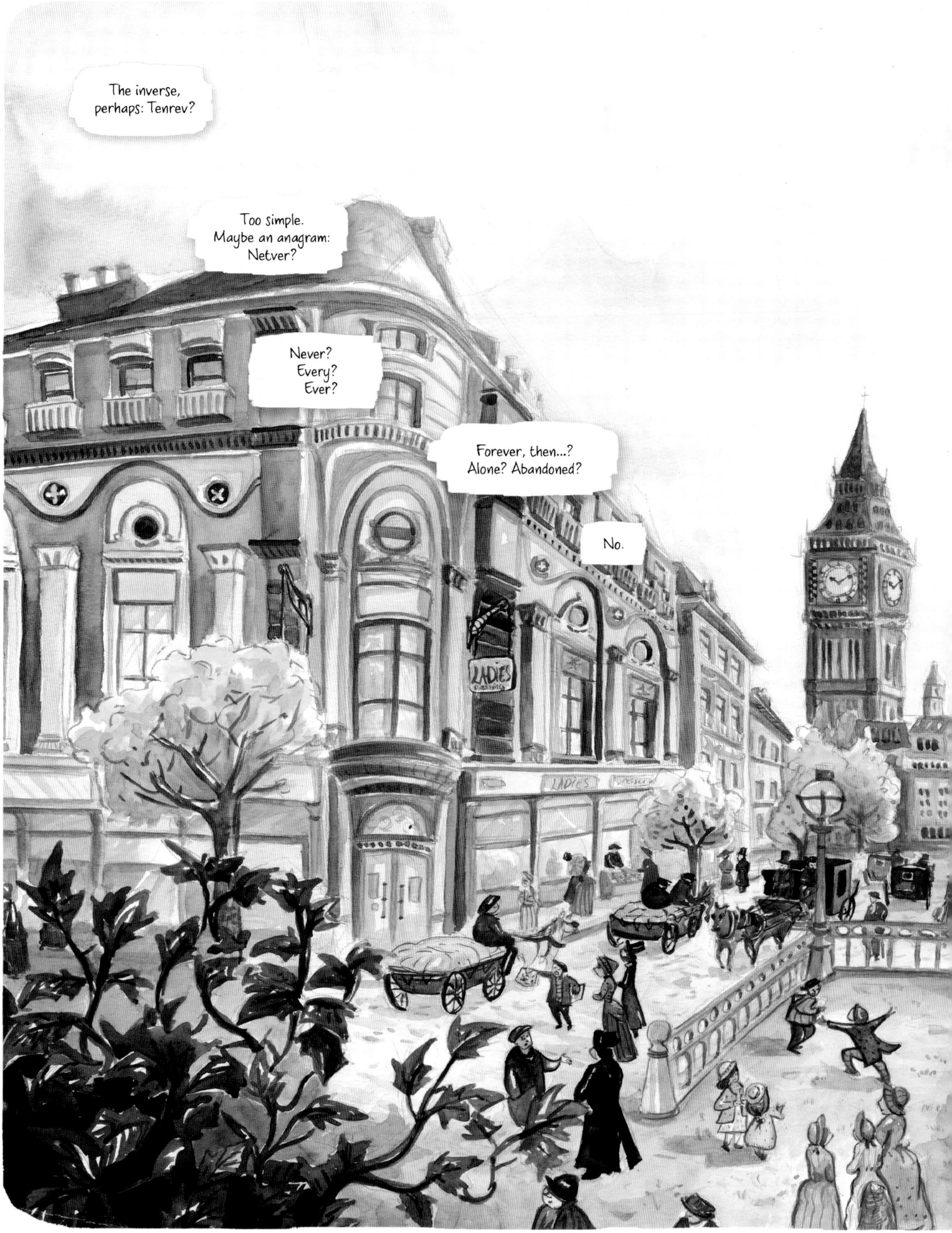
The inverse, perhaps: Tenrev?
Too simple. Maybe an anagram: Netver?
Never? Every? Ever?
Forever, then...? Alone? Abandoned?
No.

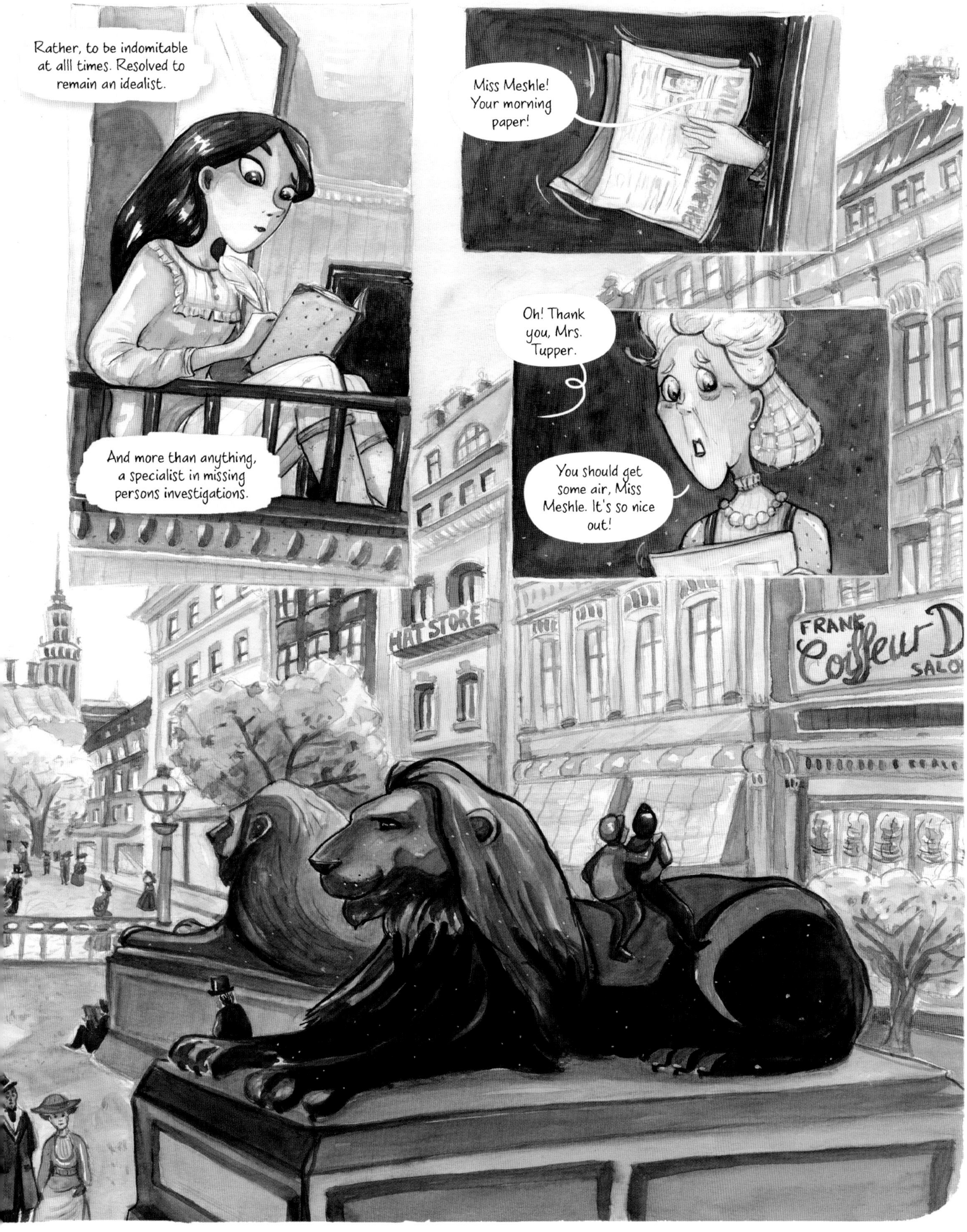
Rather, to be indomitable at alll times. Resolved to remain an idealist.
And more than anything, a specialist in missing persons investigations.
Miss Meshle! Your morning paper!
Oh! Thank you, Mrs. Tupper.
You should get some air, Miss Meshle. It's so nice out!
HAT STORE
FRANK
Coiffeur D
SALO

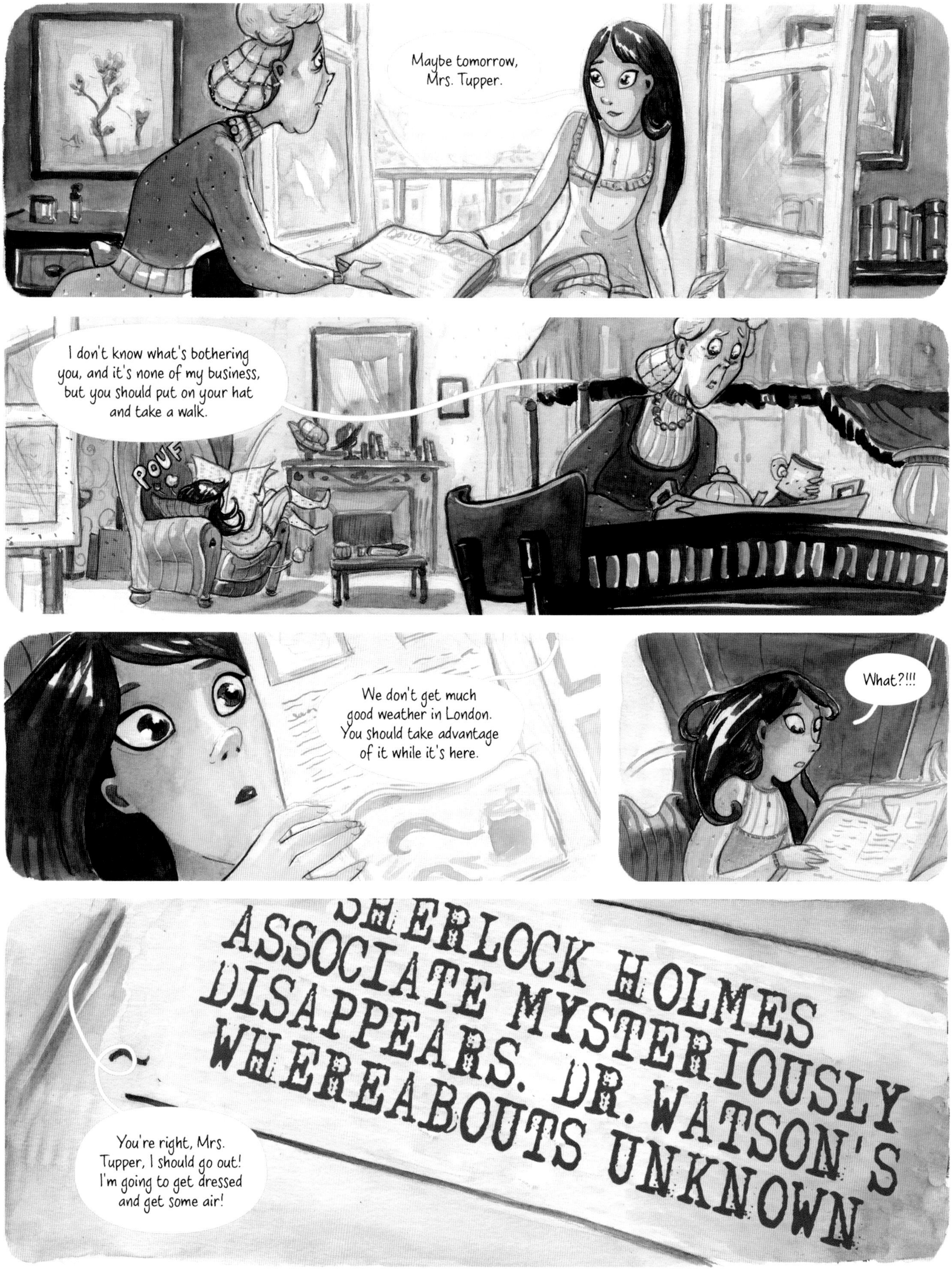
Maybe tomorrow, Mrs. Tupper.
I don't know what's bothering you, and it's none of my business, but you should put on your hat and take a walk.
POUF
We don't get much good weather in London. You should take advantage of it while it's here.
What?!!!
SHERLOCK HOLMES ASSOCIATE MYSTERIOUSLY DISAPPEARS. DR. WATSON'S WHEREABOUTS UNKNOWN
You're right, Mrs. Tupper, I should go out! I'm going to get dressed and get some air!

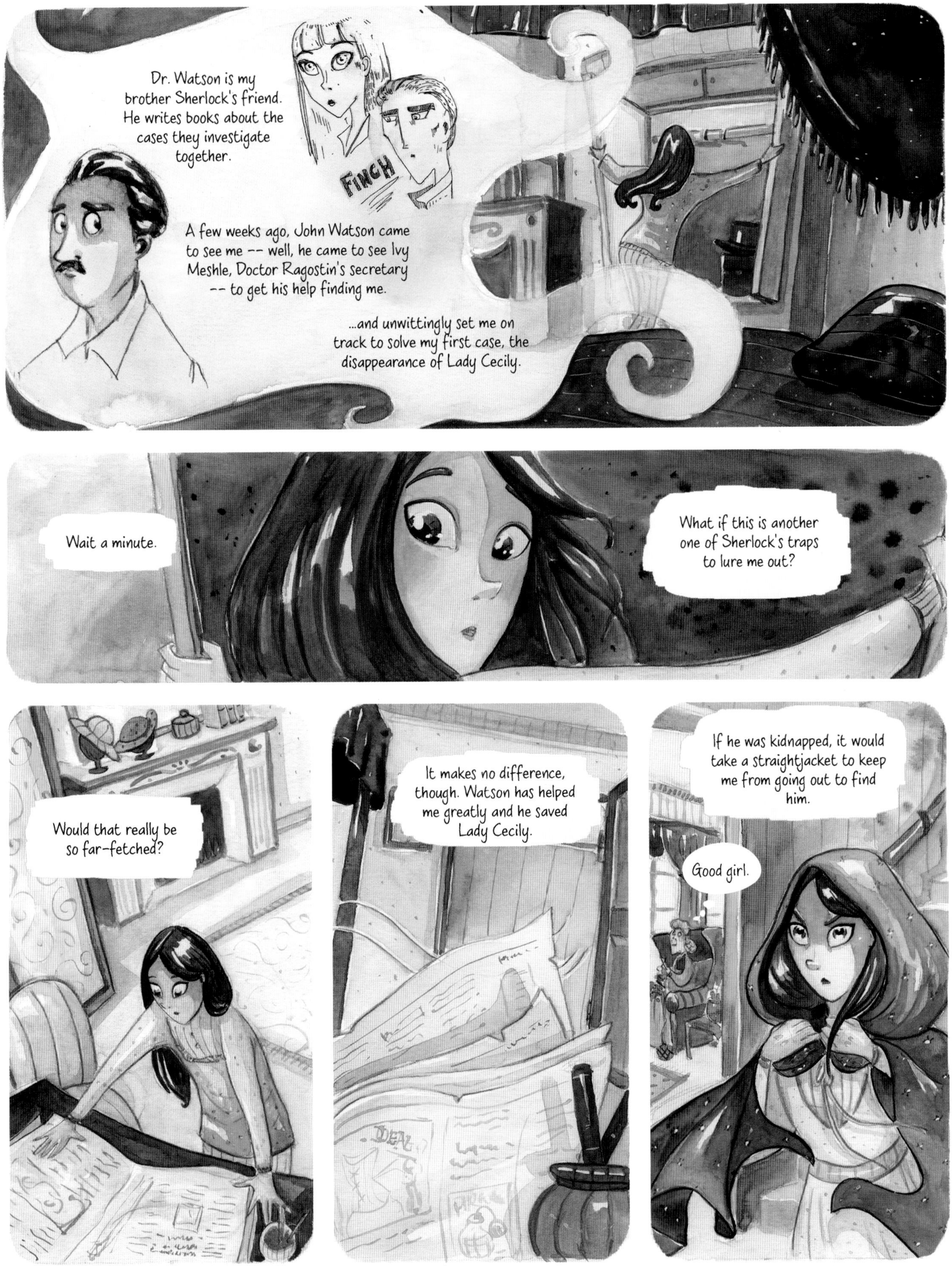
Dr. Watson is my brother Sherlock's friend. He writes books about the cases they investigate together.
FINCH
A few weeks ago, John Watson came to see me -- well, he came to see Ivy Meshle, Doctor Ragostin's secretary -- to get his help finding me.
...and unwittingly set me on track to solve my first case, the disappearance of Lady Cecily.
Wait a minute.
What if this is another one of Sherlock's traps to lure me out?
Would that really be so far-fetched?
It makes no difference, though. Watson has helped me greatly and he saved Lady Cecily.
If he was kidnapped, it would take a straightjacket to keep me from going out to find him.
Good girl.

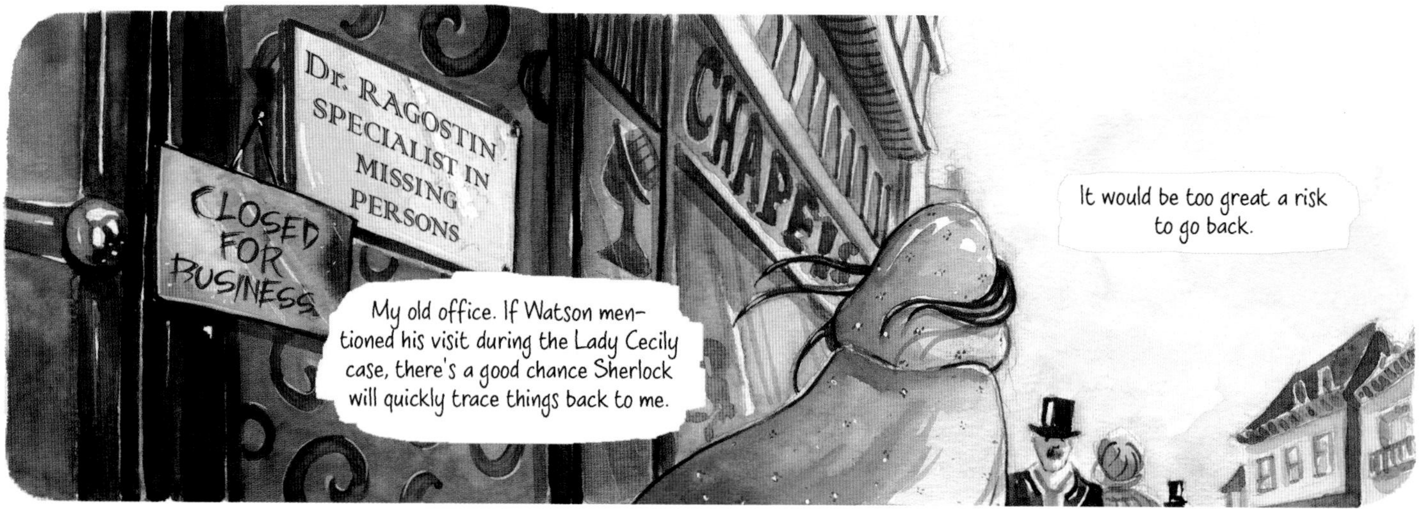
Dr. RAGOSTIN SPECIALIST IN MISSING PERSONS
CLOSED FOR BUSINESS
CHAPE
My old office. If Watson mentioned his visit during the Lady Cecily case, there's a good chance Sherlock will quickly trace things back to me.
It would be too great a risk to go back.

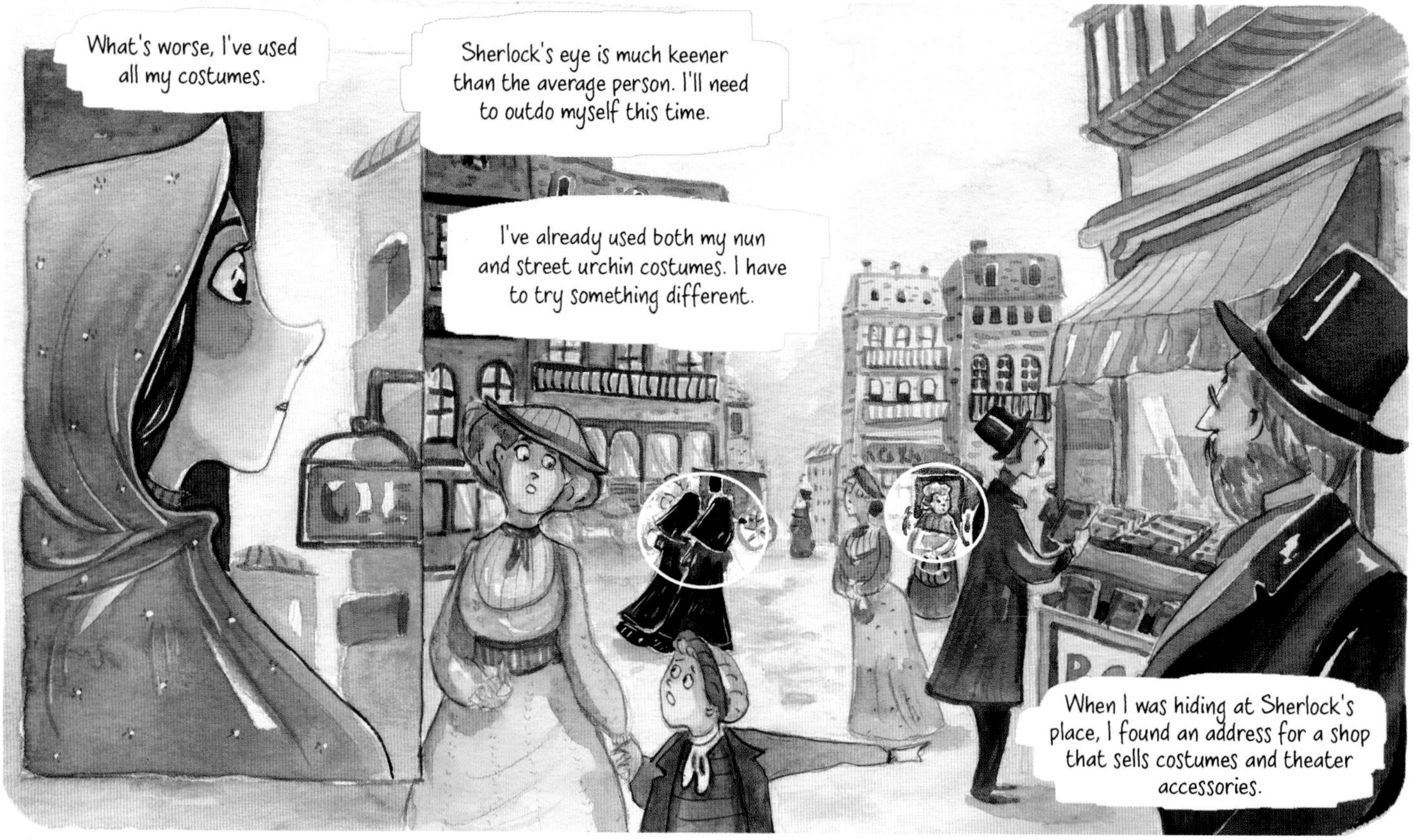
What's worse, I've used all my costumes.
Sherlock's eye is much keener than the average person. I'll need to outdo myself this time.
I've already used both my nun and street urchin costumes. I have to try something different.
When I was hiding at Sherlock's place, I found an address for a shop that sells costumes and theater accessories.

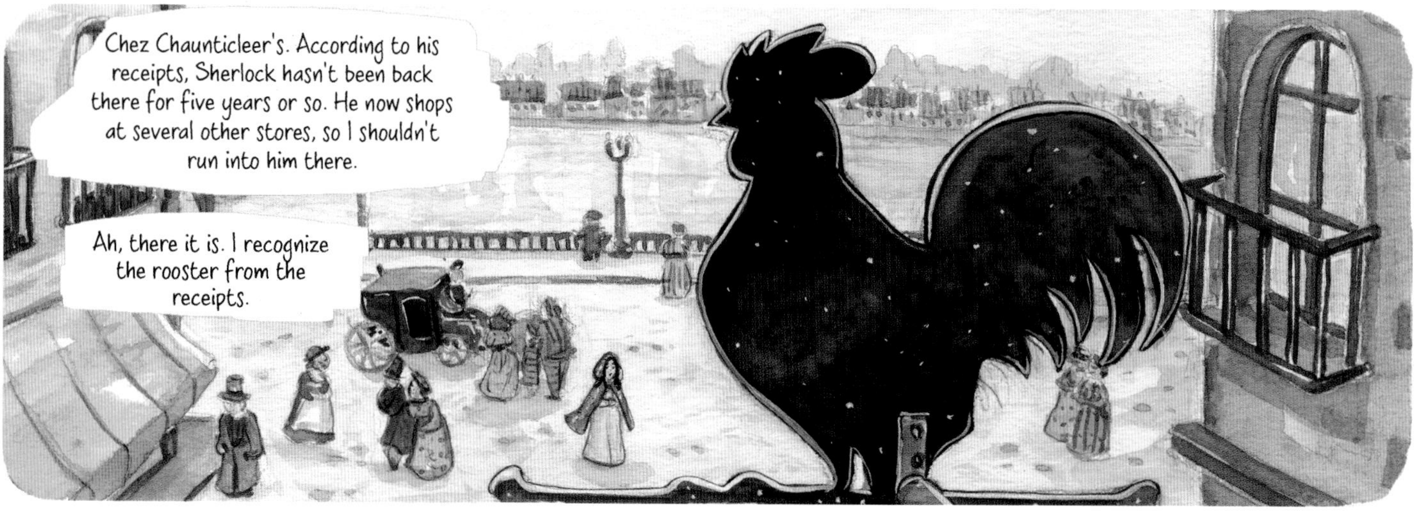
Chez Chaunticleer's. According to his receipts, Sherlock hasn't been back there for five years or so. He now shops at several other stores, so I shouldn't run into him there.
Ah, there it is. I recognize the rooster from the receipts.

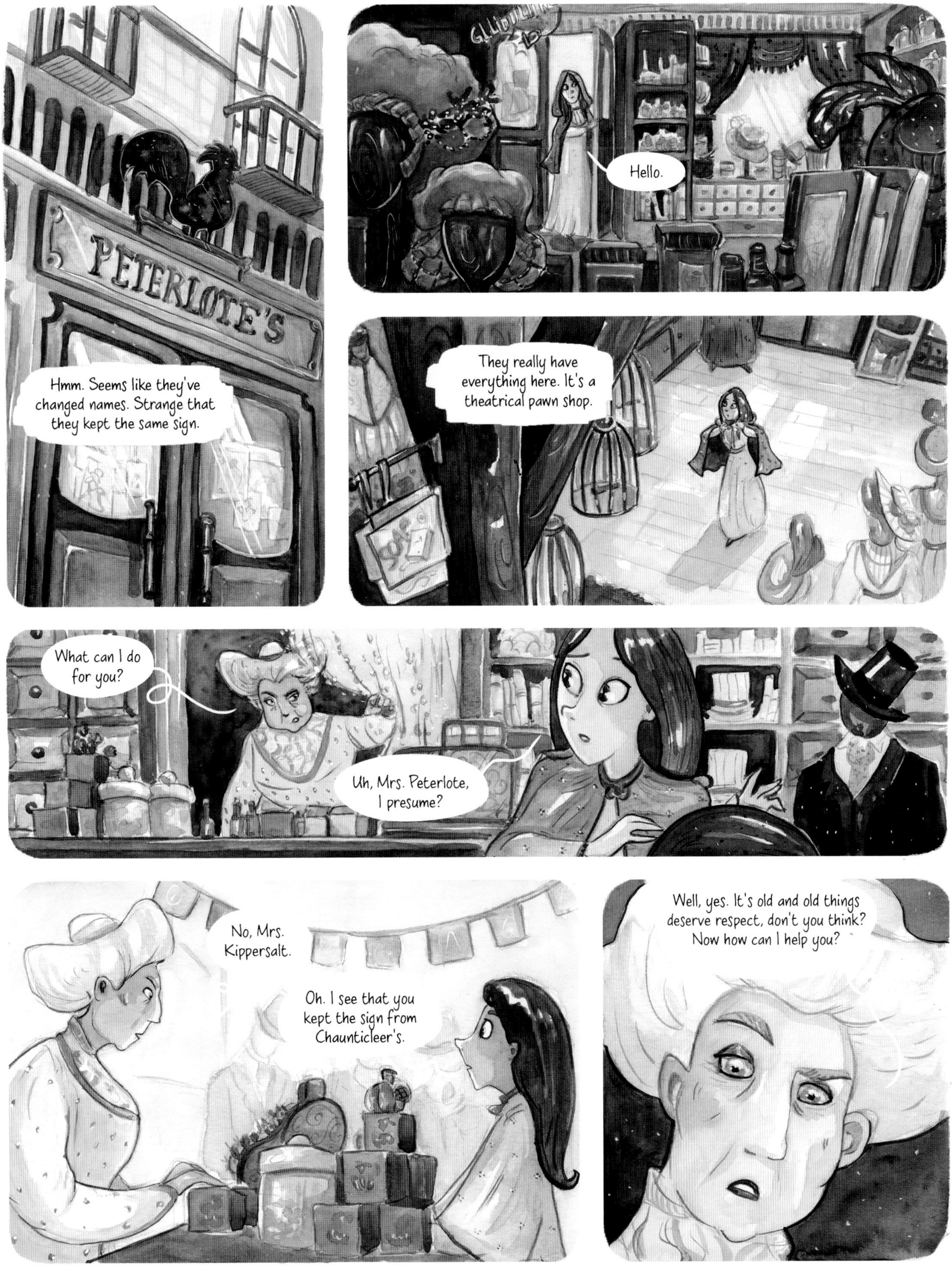
PETERLOTE'S
Hmm. Seems like they've changed names. Strange that they kept the same sign.
GLLIDIDLINK
Hello.
They really have everything here. It's a theatrical pawn shop.
What can I do for you?
Uh, Mrs. Peterlote, I presume?
No, Mrs. Kippersalt.
Oh. I see that you kept the sign from Chaunticleer's.
Well, yes. It's old and old things deserve respect, don't you think? Now how can I help you?

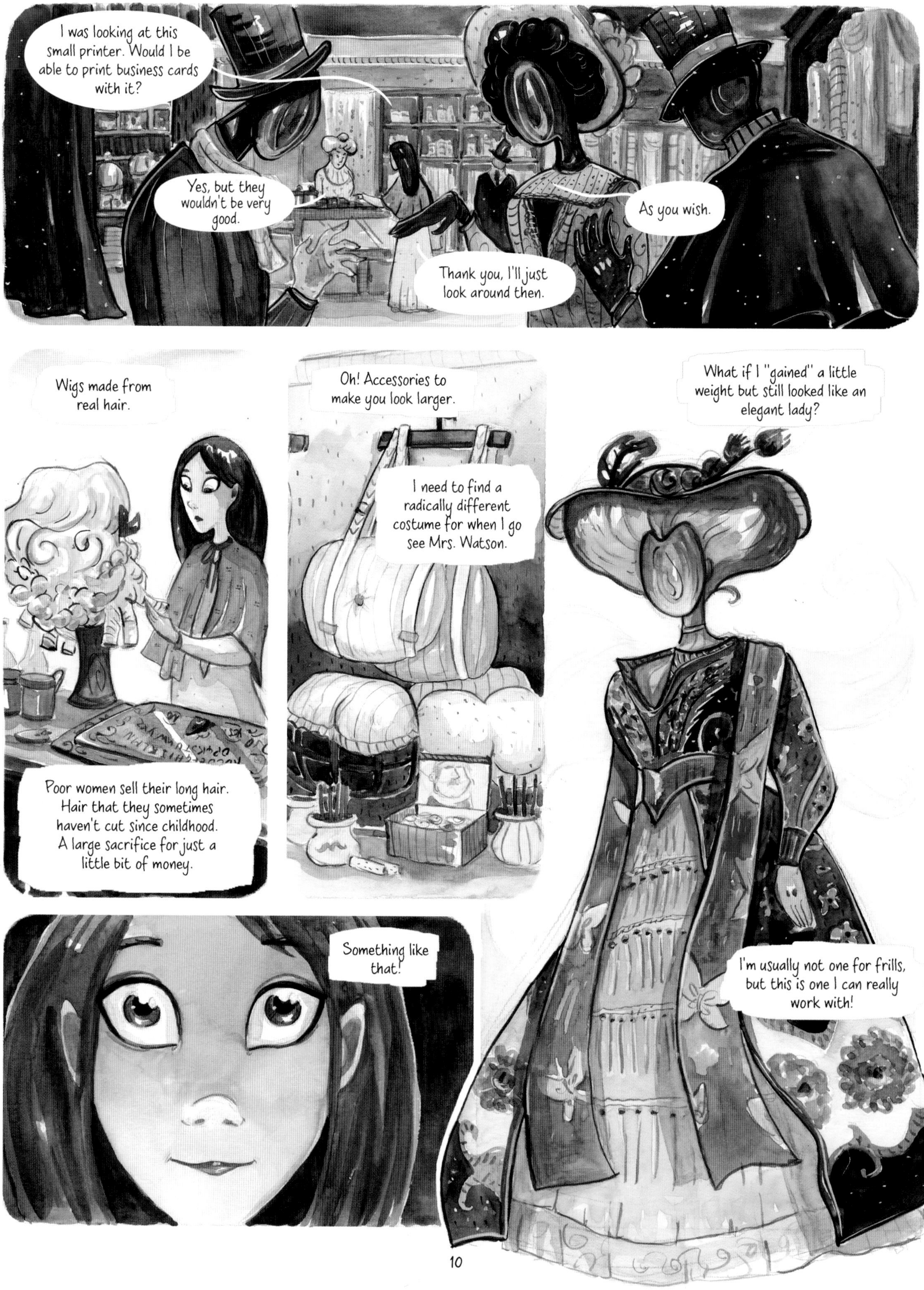
I was looking at this small printer. Would I be able to print business cards with it?
Yes, but they wouldn't be very good.
As you wish.
Thank you, I'll just look around then.
Wigs made from real hair.
Poor women sell their long hair. Hair that they sometimes haven't cut since childhood. A large sacrifice for just a little bit of money.
Oh! Accessories to make you look larger.
I need to find a radically different costume for when I go see Mrs. Watson.
What if I "gained" a little weight but still looked like an elegant lady?
Something like that!
I'm usually not one for frills, but this is one I can really work with!

The next day.

I hope Mrs. Watson will see me, after I've gone to so much trouble.

Whitening my skin, using some padding here and there, and thousands of petticoats!

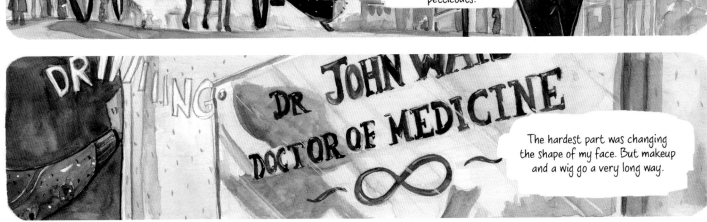

DR JOHN WA[...] DOCTOR OF MEDICINE

The hardest part was changing the shape of my face. But makeup and a wig go a very long way.

Miss Viola Eversea.

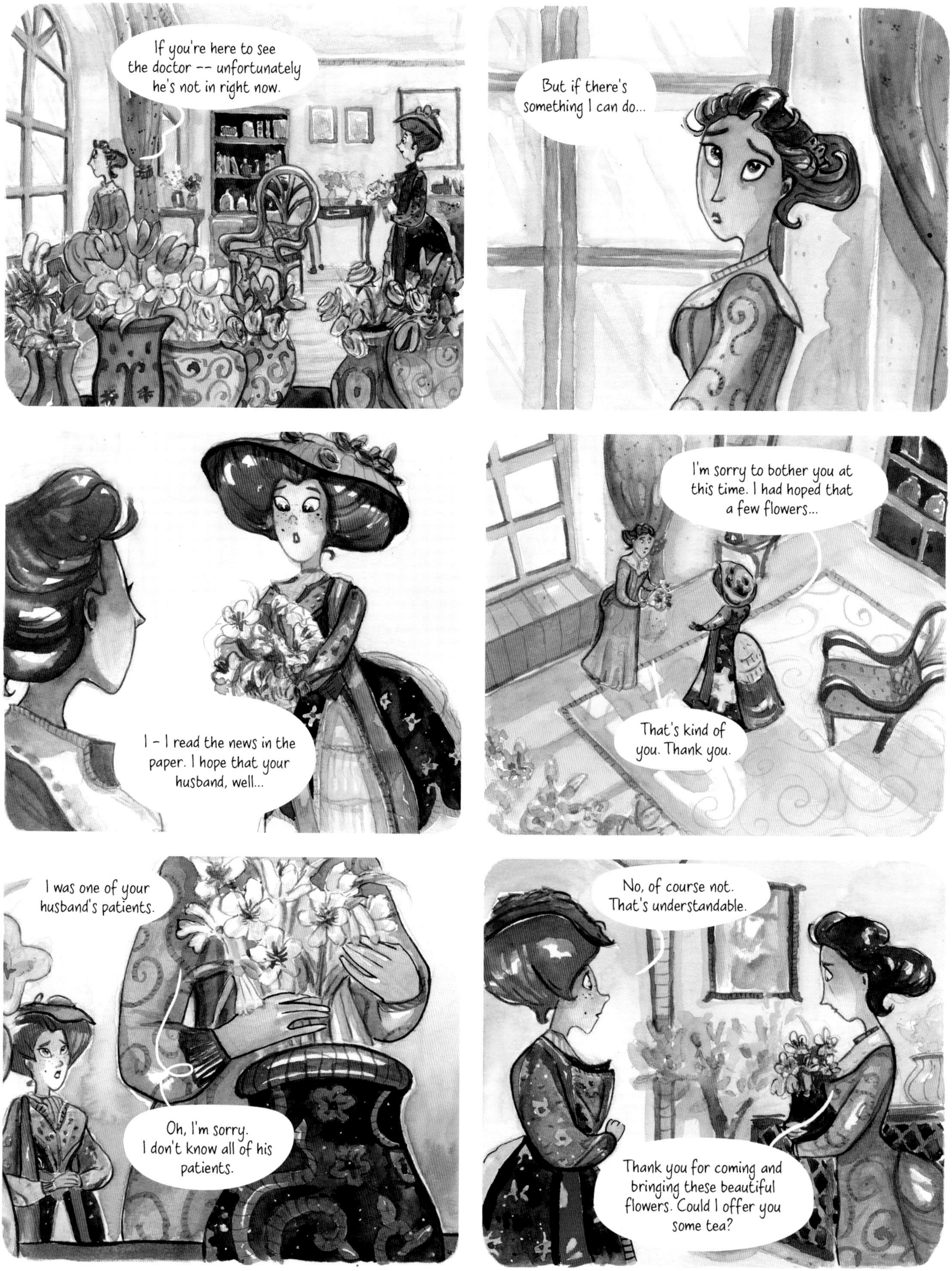
If you're here to see the doctor -- unfortunately he's not in right now.
But if there's something I can do...
I – I read the news in the paper. I hope that your husband, well...
I'm sorry to bother you at this time. I had hoped that a few flowers...
That's kind of you. Thank you.
I was one of your husband's patients.
Oh, I'm sorry. I don't know all of his patients.
No, of course not. That's understandable.
Thank you for coming and bringing these beautiful flowers. Could I offer you some tea?

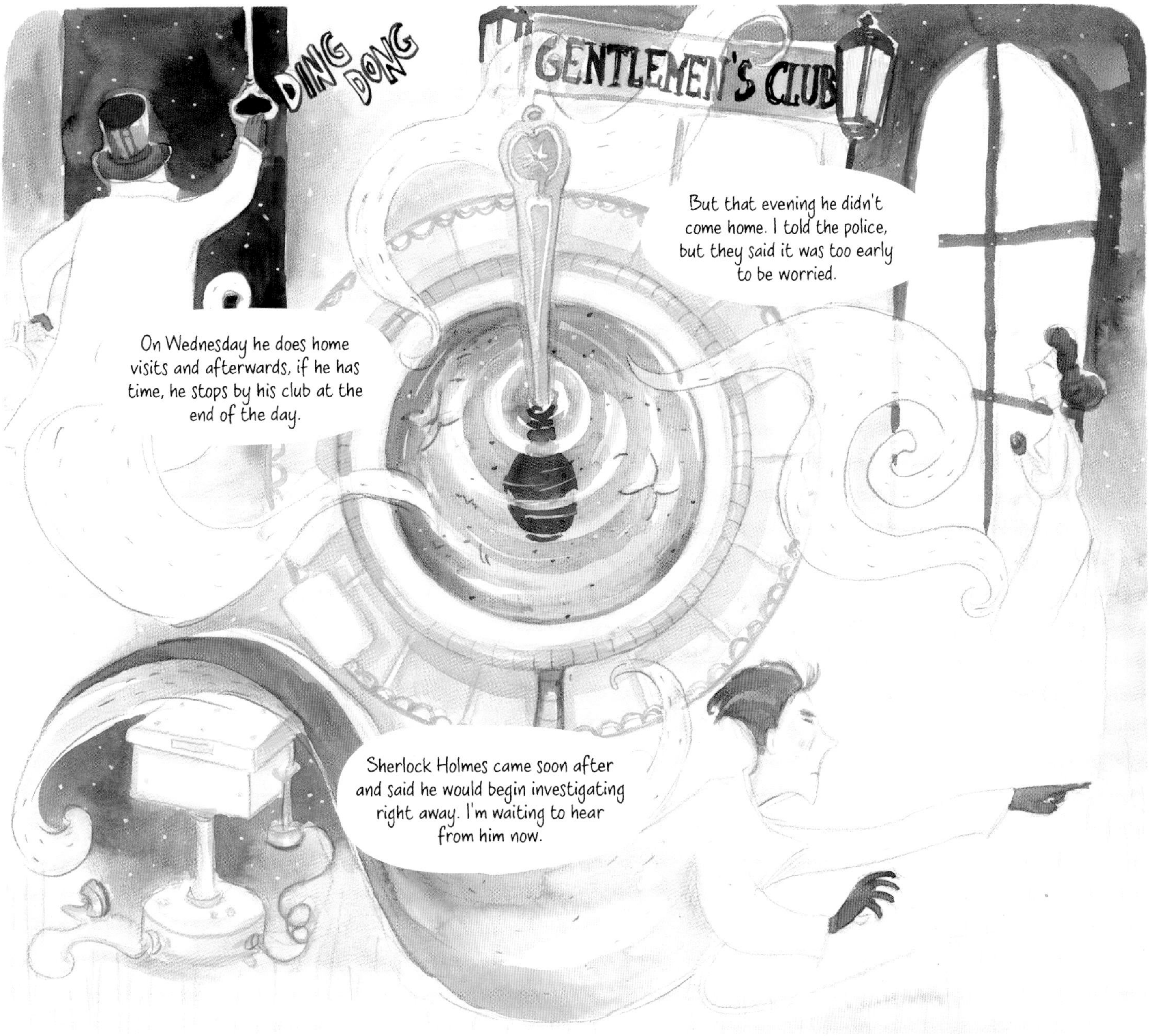
GENTLEMEN'S CLUB
DING DONG
On Wednesday he does home visits and afterwards, if he has time, he stops by his club at the end of the day.
But that evening he didn't come home. I told the police, but they said it was too early to be worried.
Sherlock Holmes came soon after and said he would begin investigating right away. I'm waiting to hear from him now.

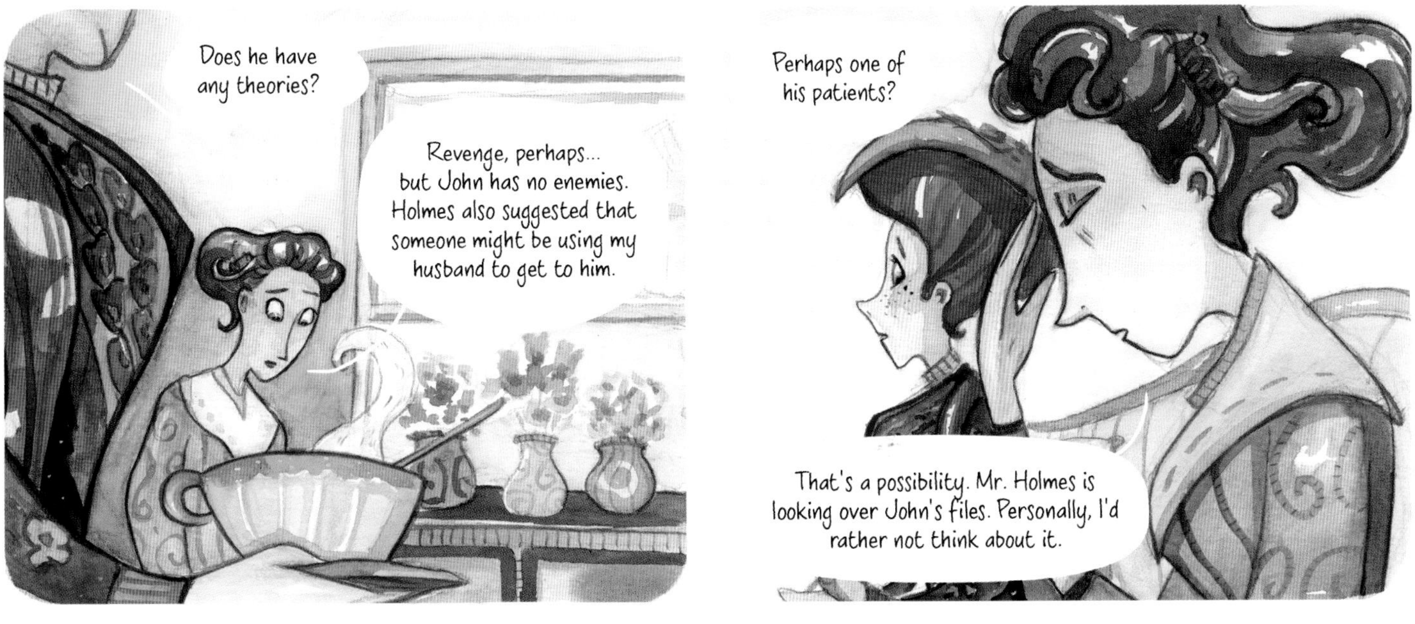
Does he have any theories?
Revenge, perhaps... but John has no enemies. Holmes also suggested that someone might be using my husband to get to him.
Perhaps one of his patients?
That's a possibility. Mr. Holmes is looking over John's files. Personally, I'd rather not think about it.

You've received a lot of beautiful bouquets.

It's a kind gesture, considering I barely know many of the people.

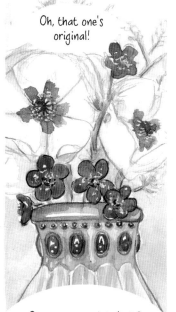

Oh, that one's original!

Oh, yes, unusual, isn't it? The poppies here are red, not white, and hawthorn, which is usually red, is white. I'm not familiar with that little sprig of green, though.

It's asparagus. Asparagus leaves.

Really? That's surprising for a bouquet. How did you recognize it?

My mother was a botanist. Mrs. Watson. Do you understand flower symbology?

Not really, no. Don't poppies symbolize comfort and hawthorns, hope?

Red poppies, yes, but white poppies symbolize sleep.

Oh. Speaking of which, sleep would probably do me some good.

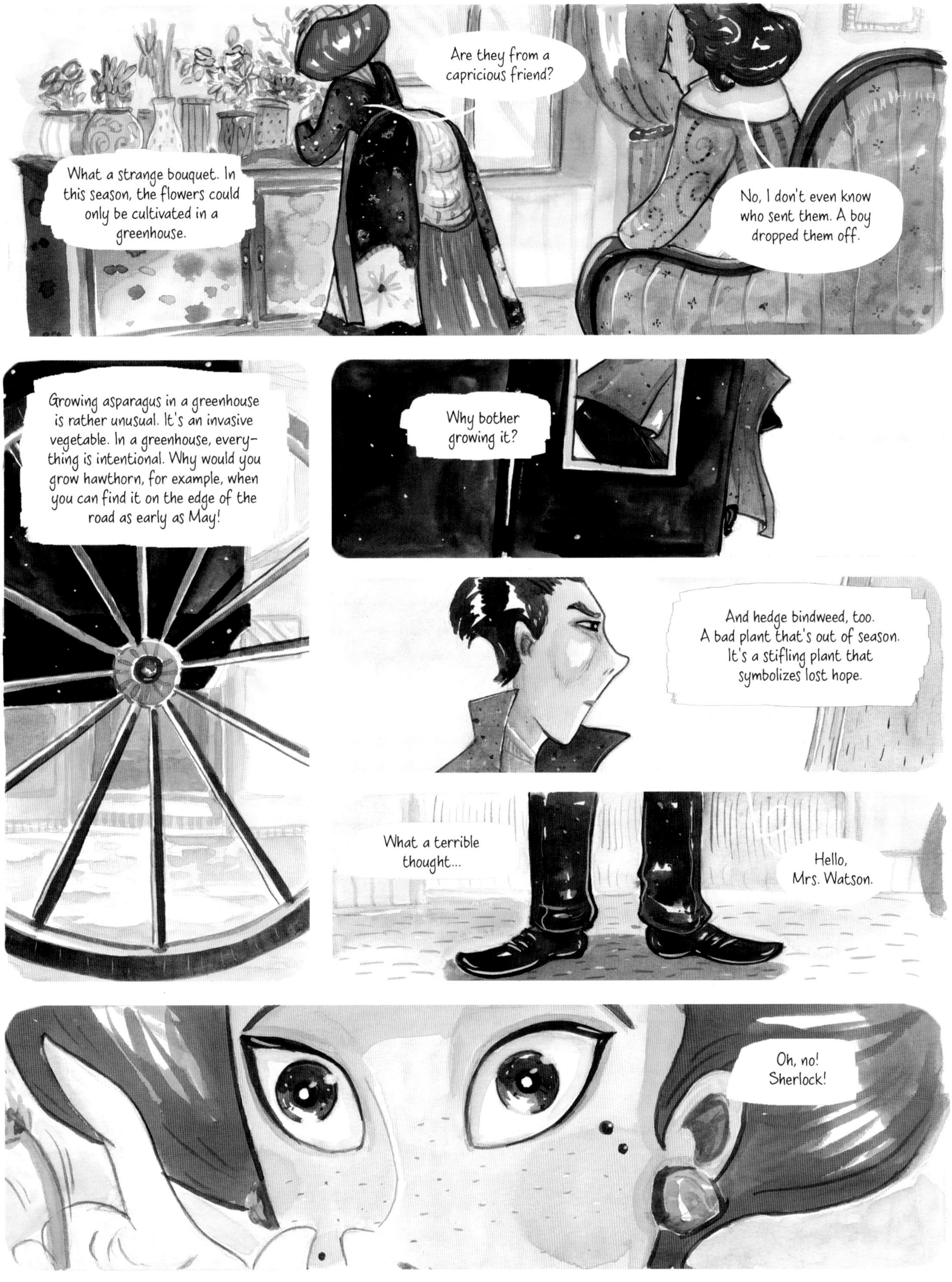
Are they from a capricious friend?
What a strange bouquet. In this season, the flowers could only be cultivated in a greenhouse.
No, I don't even know who sent them. A boy dropped them off.
Growing asparagus in a greenhouse is rather unusual. It's an invasive vegetable. In a greenhouse, everything is intentional. Why would you grow hawthorn, for example, when you can find it on the edge of the road as early as May!
Why bother growing it?
And hedge bindweed, too. A bad plant that's out of season. It's a stifling plant that symbolizes lost hope.
What a terrible thought...
Hello, Mrs. Watson.
Oh, no! Sherlock!

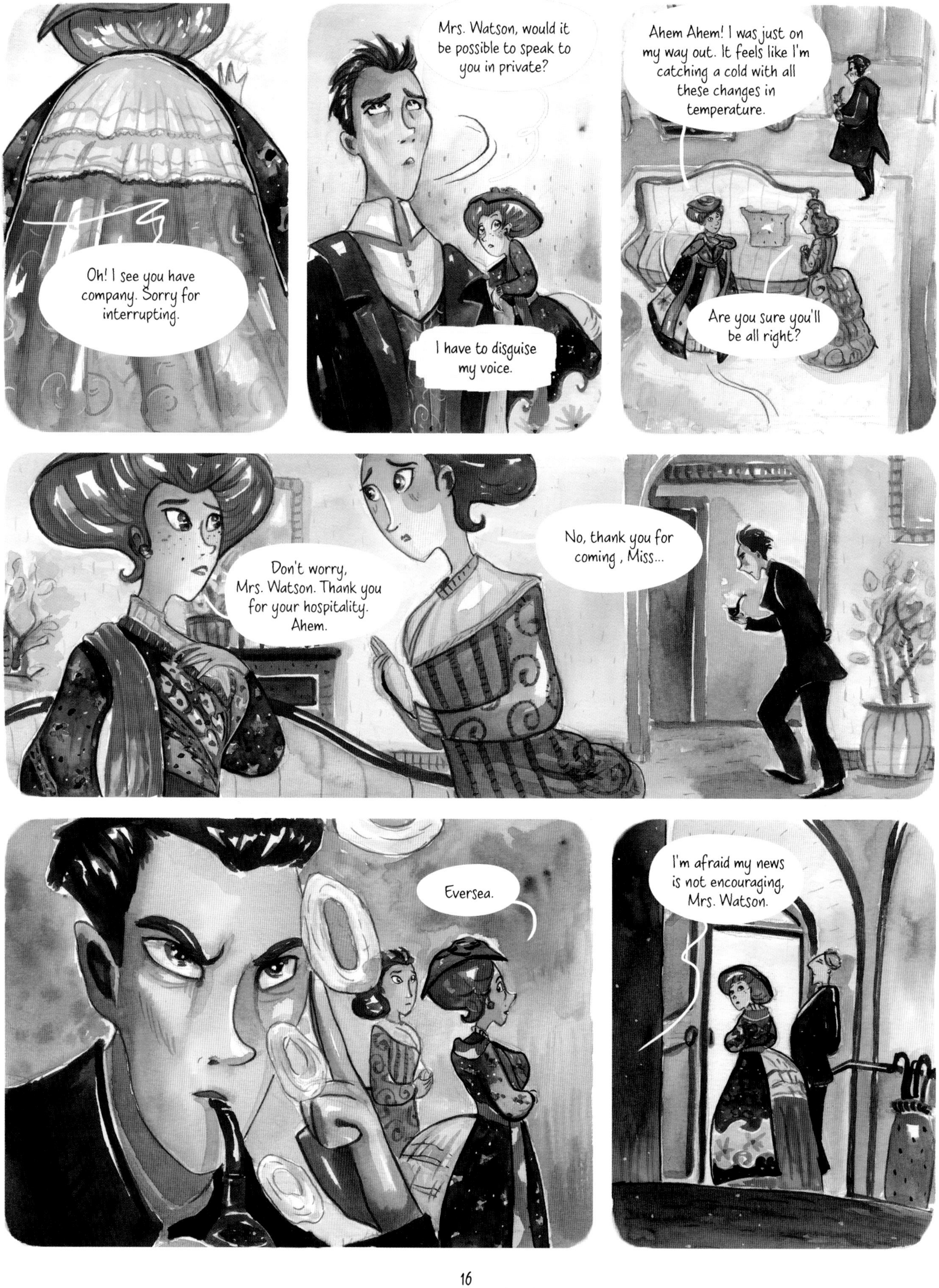
Oh! I see you have company. Sorry for interrupting.
Mrs. Watson, would it be possible to speak to you in private?
I have to disguise my voice.
Ahem Ahem! I was just on my way out. It feels like I'm catching a cold with all these changes in temperature.
Are you sure you'll be all right?
Don't worry, Mrs. Watson. Thank you for your hospitality. Ahem.
No, thank you for coming , Miss...
Eversea.
I'm afraid my news is not encouraging, Mrs. Watson.

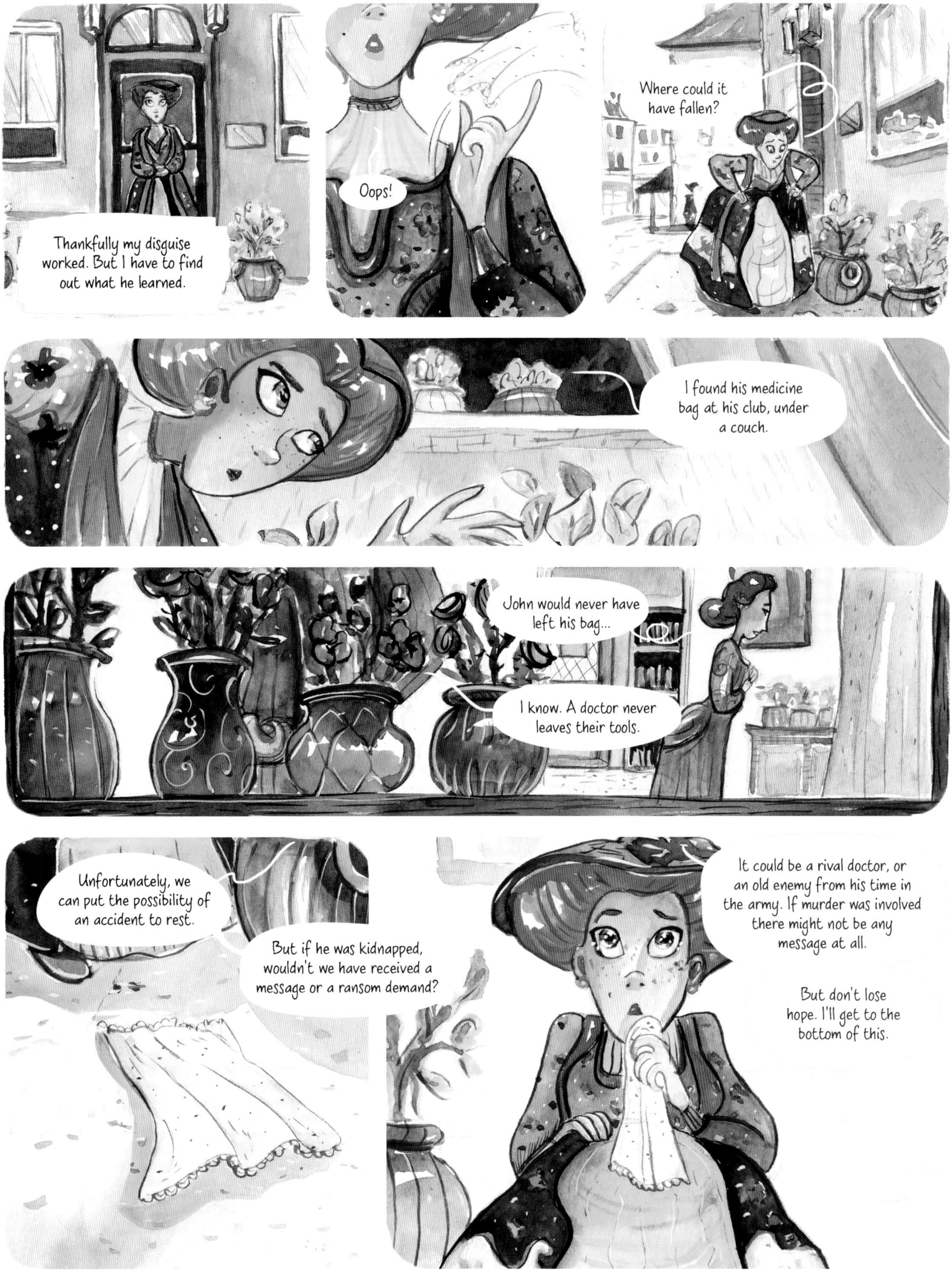
Thankfully my disguise worked. But I have to find out what he learned.
Oops!
Where could it have fallen?
I found his medicine bag at his club, under a couch.
John would never have left his bag...
I know. A doctor never leaves their tools.
Unfortunately, we can put the possibility of an accident to rest.
But if he was kidnapped, wouldn't we have received a message or a ransom demand?
It could be a rival doctor, or an old enemy from his time in the army. If murder was involved there might not be any message at all.
But don't lose hope. I'll get to the bottom of this.

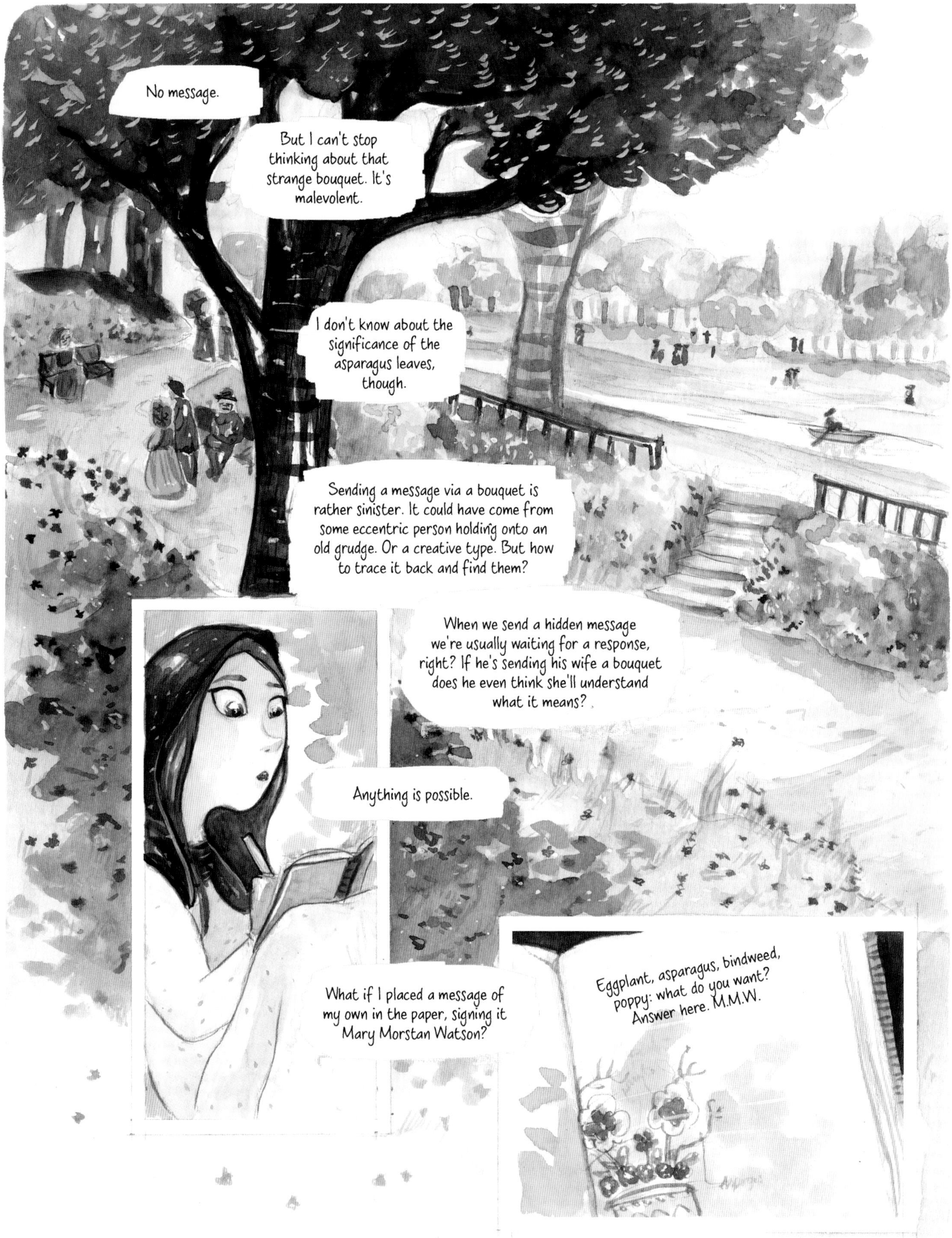
No message.
But I can't stop thinking about that strange bouquet. It's malevolent.
I don't know about the significance of the asparagus leaves, though.
Sending a message via a bouquet is rather sinister. It could have come from some eccentric person holding onto an old grudge. Or a creative type. But how to trace it back and find them?
When we send a hidden message we're usually waiting for a response, right? If he's sending his wife a bouquet does he even think she'll understand what it means?
Anything is possible.
What if I placed a message of my own in the paper, signing it Mary Morstan Watson?
Eggplant, asparagus, bindweed, poppy: what do you want? Answer here. M.M.W.

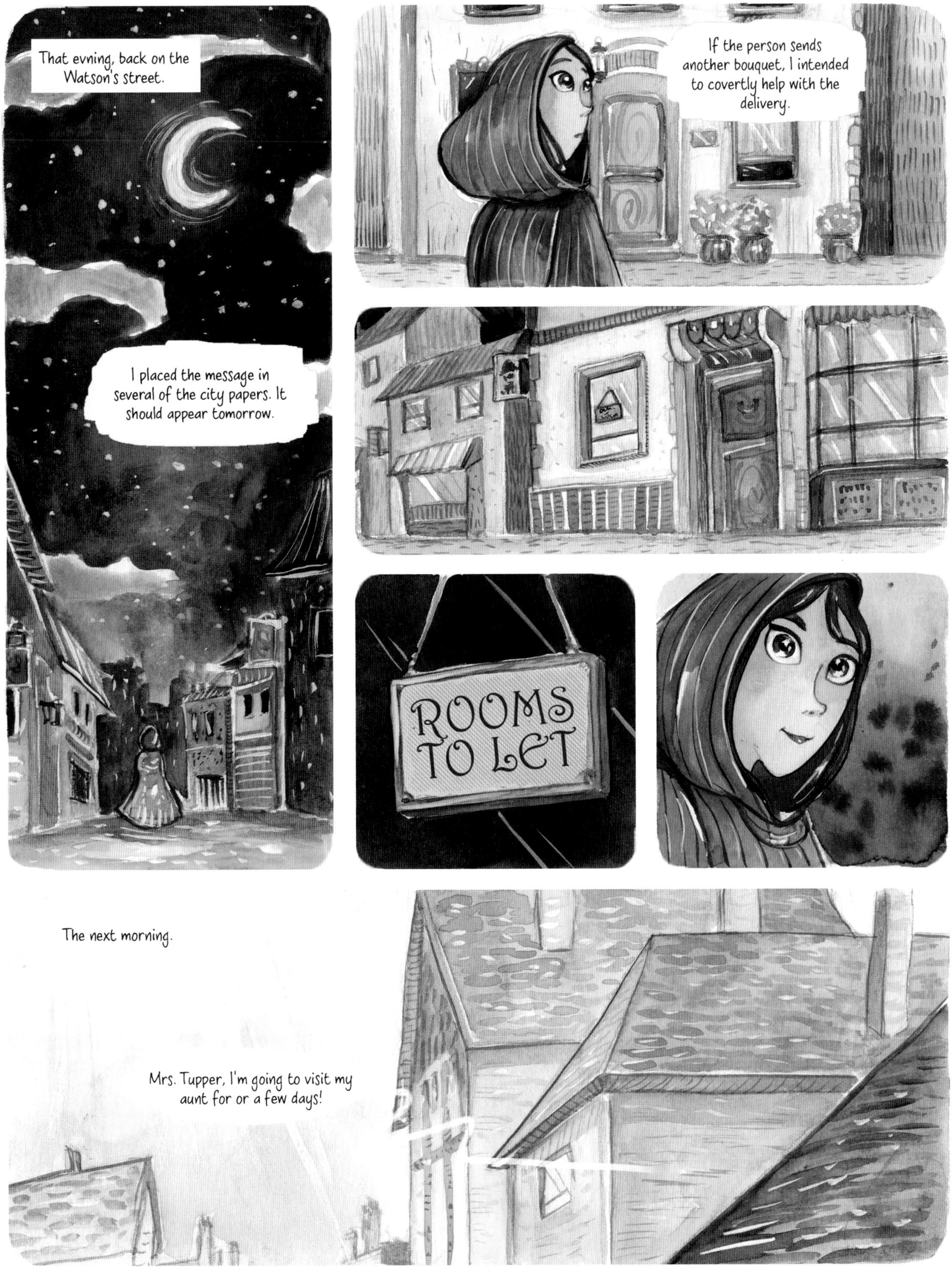
That evning, back on the Watson's street.
If the person sends another bouquet, I intended to covertly help with the delivery.
I placed the message in several of the city papers. It should appear tomorrow.
ROOMS TO LET
The next morning.
Mrs. Tupper, I'm going to visit my aunt for or a few days!

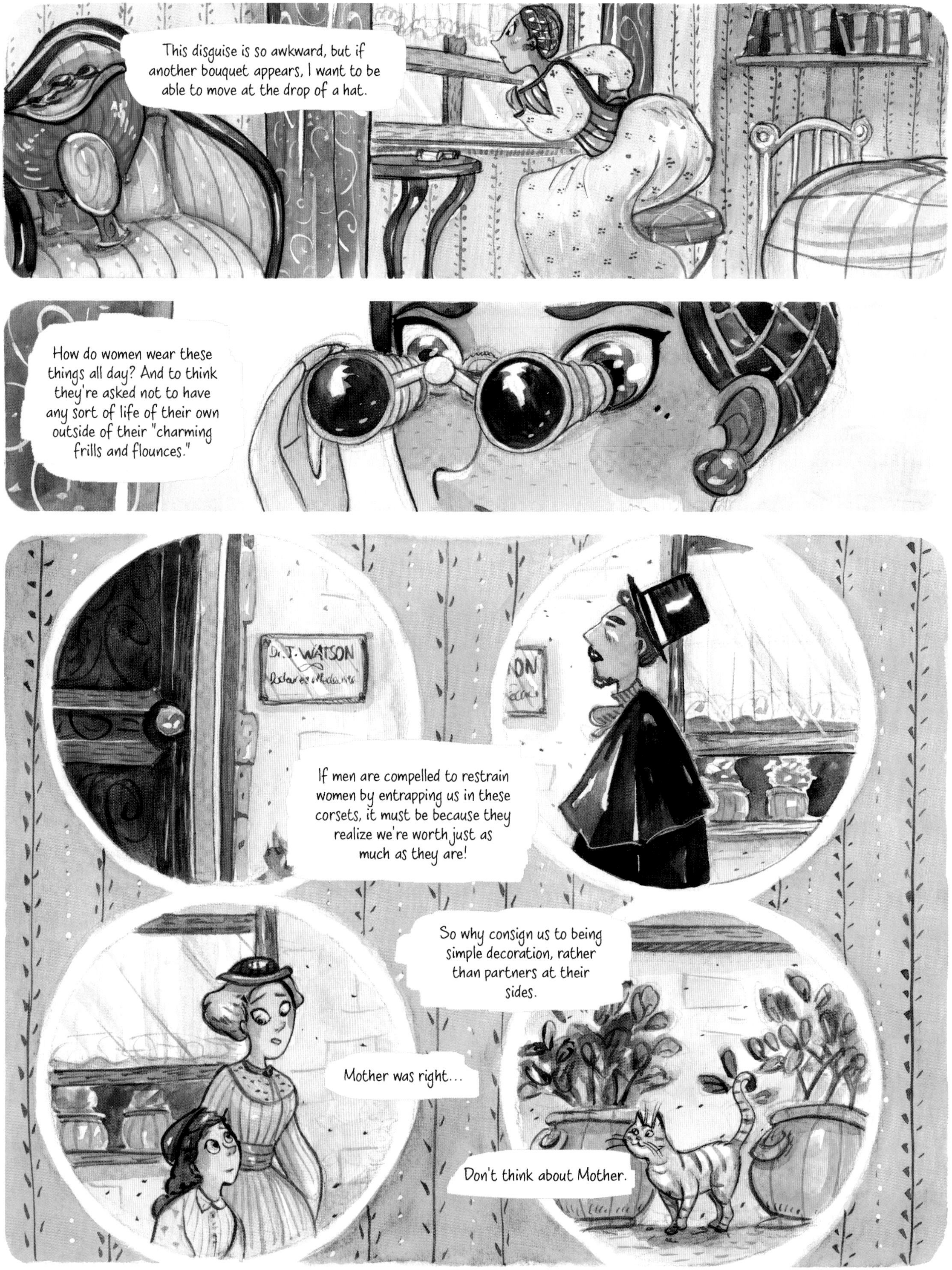
This disguise is so awkward, but if another bouquet appears, I want to be able to move at the drop of a hat.
How do women wear these things all day? And to think they're asked not to have any sort of life of their own outside of their "charming frills and flounces."
If men are compelled to restrain women by entrapping us in these corsets, it must be because they realize we're worth just as much as they are!
So why consign us to being simple decoration, rather than partners at their sides.
Mother was right...
Don't think about Mother.

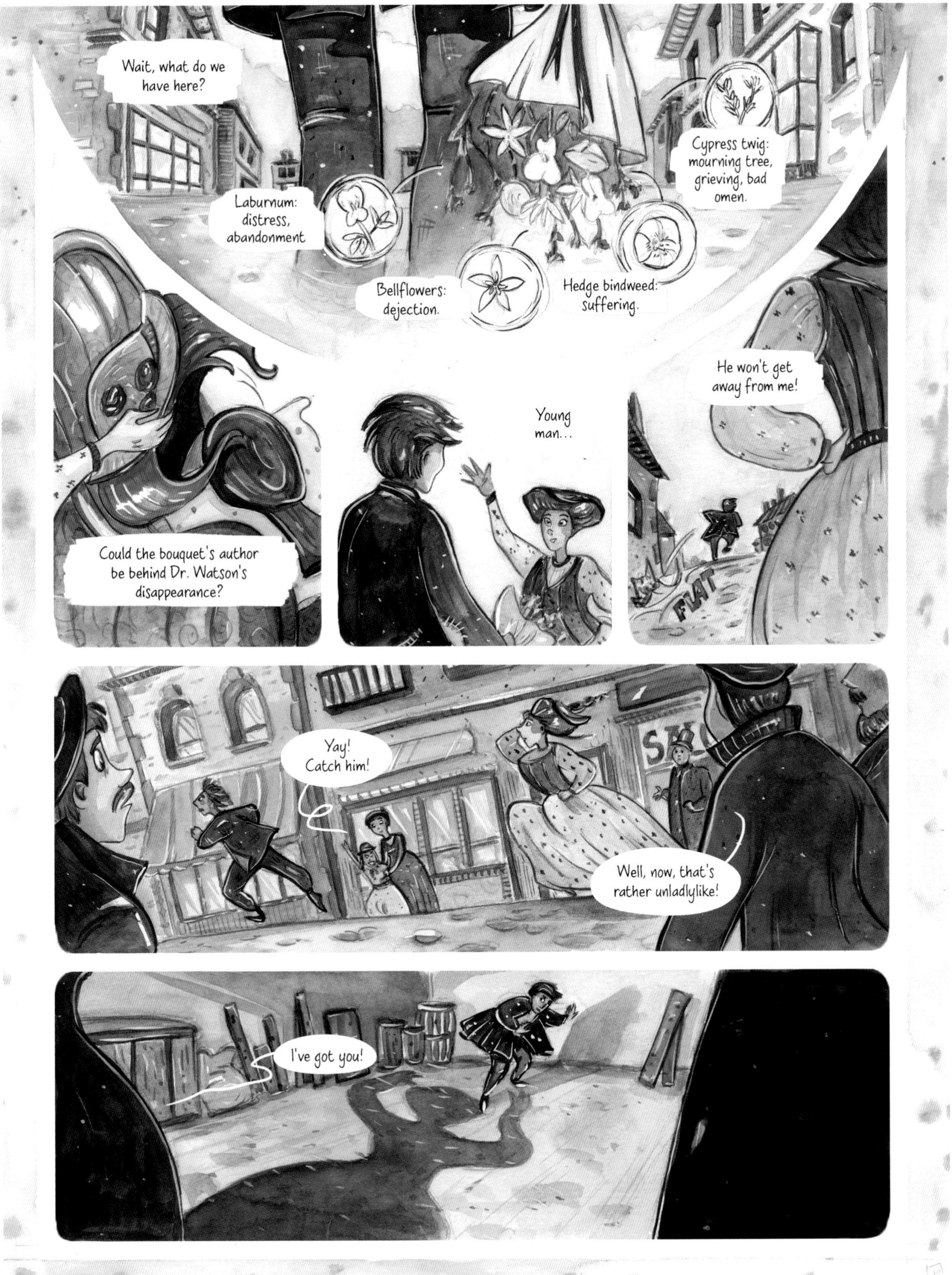
Wait, what do we have here?
Laburnum: distress, abandonment
Cypress twig: mourning tree, grieving, bad omen.
Bellflowers: dejection.
Hedge bindweed: suffering.
Could the bouquet's author be behind Dr. Watson's disappearance?
Young man...
He won't get away from me!
FLAT
Yay! Catch him!
Well, now, that's rather unladlylike!
I've got you!

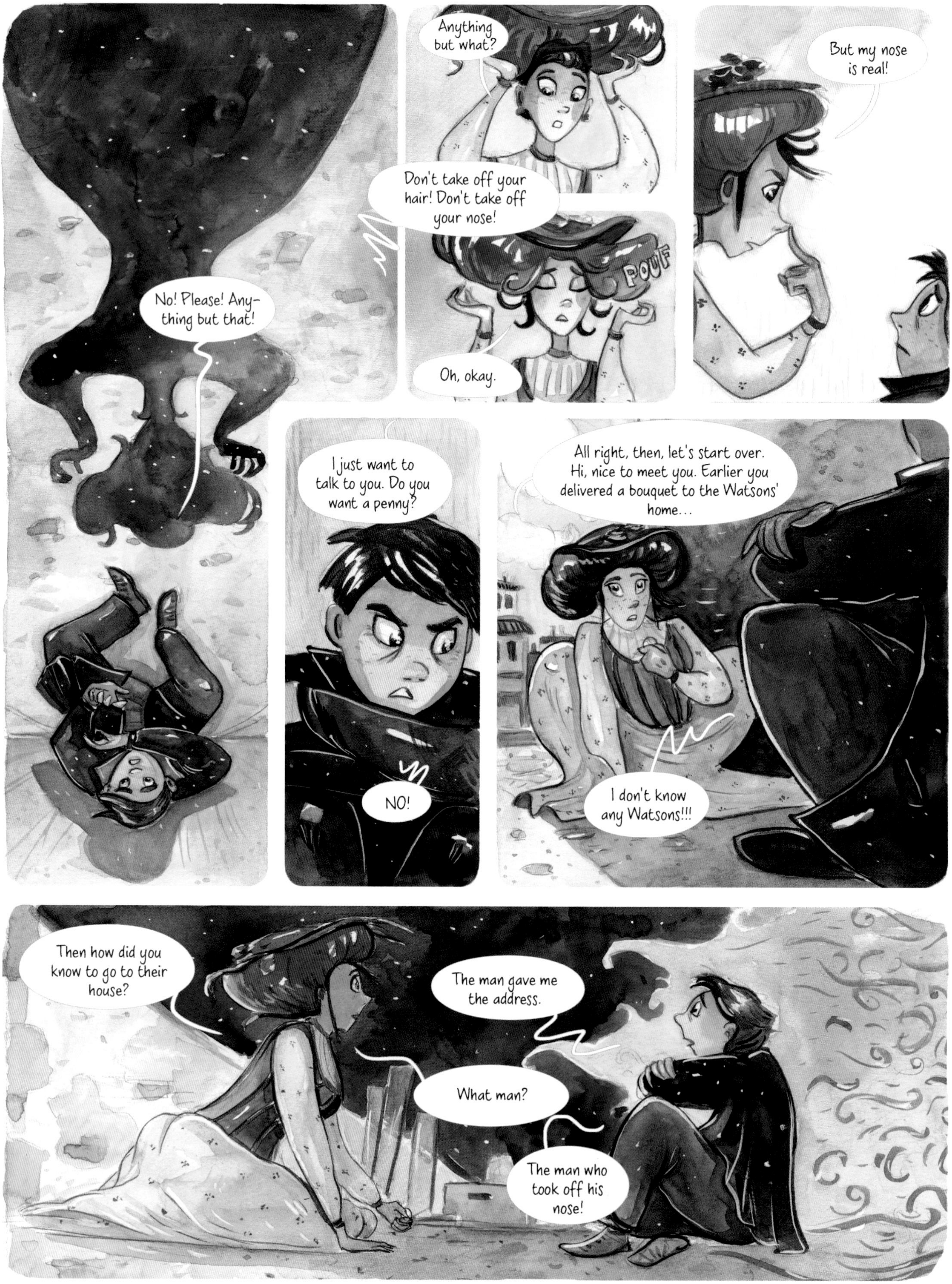
No! Please! Anything but that!
Anything but what?
Don't take off your hair! Don't take off your nose!
POUF
Oh, okay.
But my nose is real!
I just want to talk to you. Do you want a penny?
NO!
All right, then, let's start over. Hi, nice to meet you. Earlier you delivered a bouquet to the Watsons' home...
I don't know any Watsons!!!
Then how did you know to go to their house?
The man gave me the address.
What man?
The man who took off his nose!

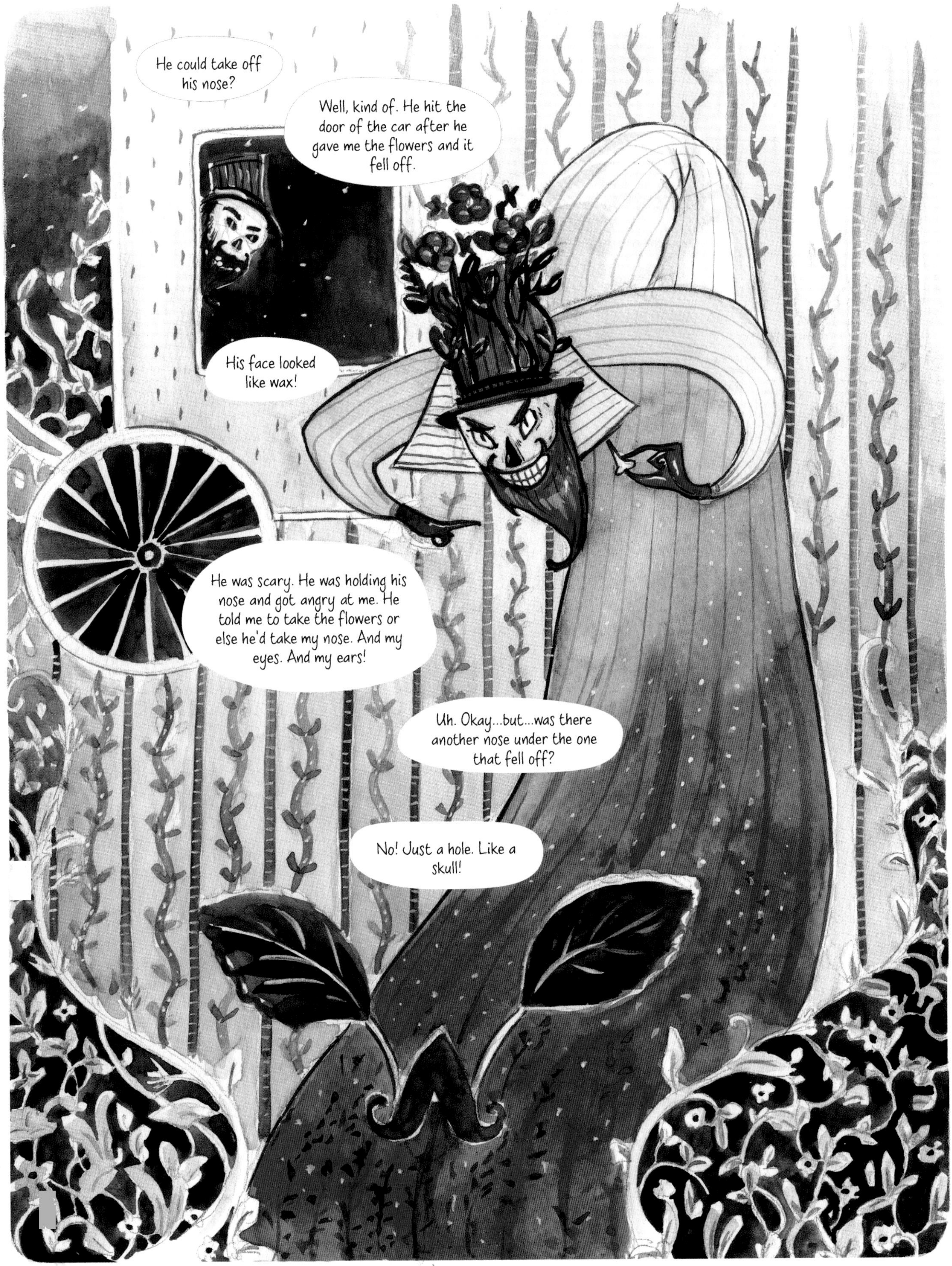
He could take off his nose?
Well, kind of. He hit the door of the car after he gave me the flowers and it fell off.
His face looked like wax!
He was scary. He was holding his nose and got angry at me. He told me to take the flowers or else he'd take my nose. And my eyes. And my ears!
Uh. Okay...but...was there another nose under the one that fell off?
No! Just a hole. Like a skull!

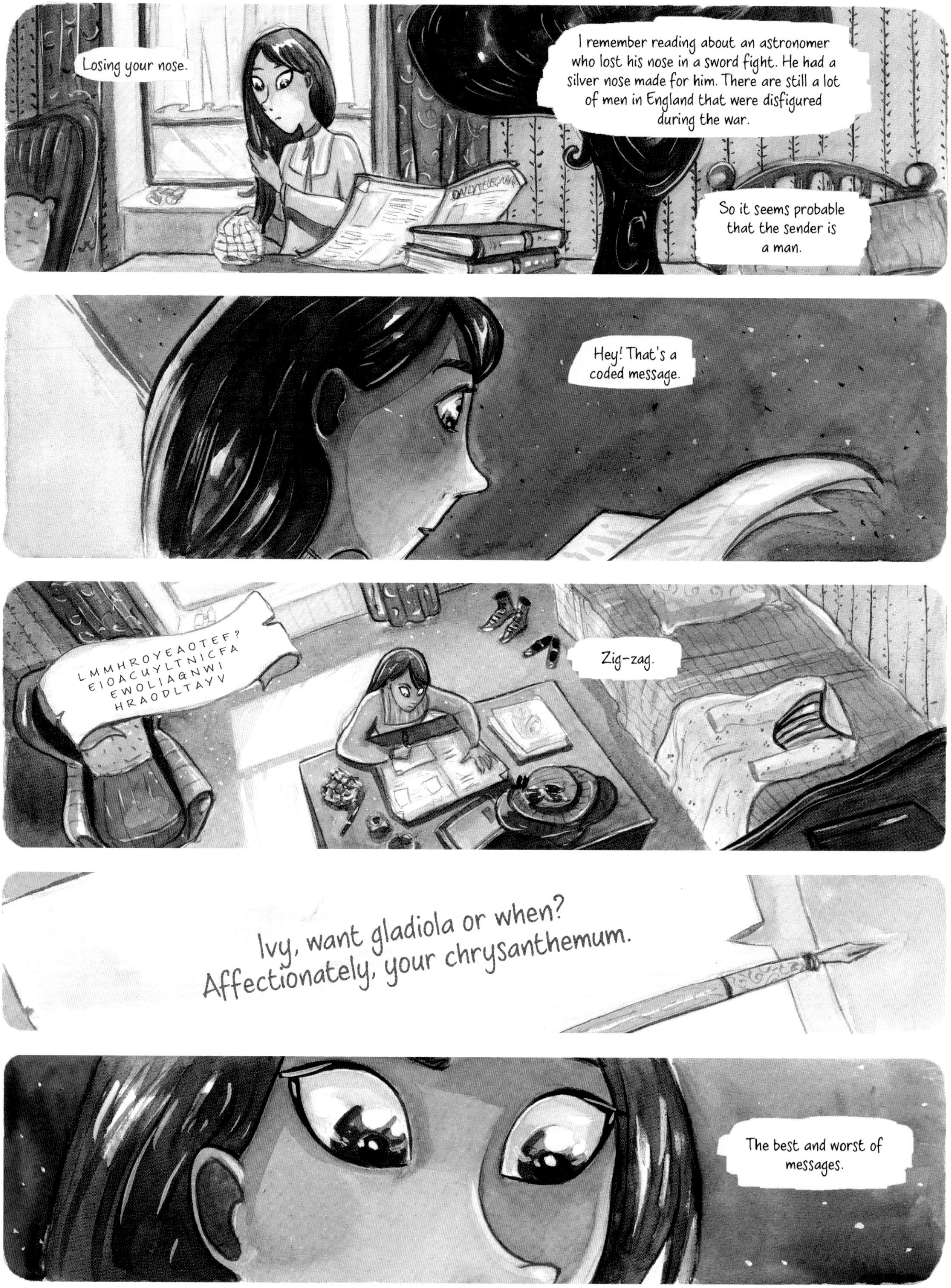
Losing your nose.
I remember reading about an astronomer who lost his nose in a sword fight. He had a silver nose made for him. There are still a lot of men in England that were disfigured during the war.
So it seems probable that the sender is a man.
Hey! That's a coded message.
LMMHROYEAOTEF?
EIOACUYLTNICFA
EWOLIAGNWI
HRAODLTAYV
Zig-zag.
Ivy, want gladiola or when?
Affectionately, your chrysanthemum.
The best and worst of messages.

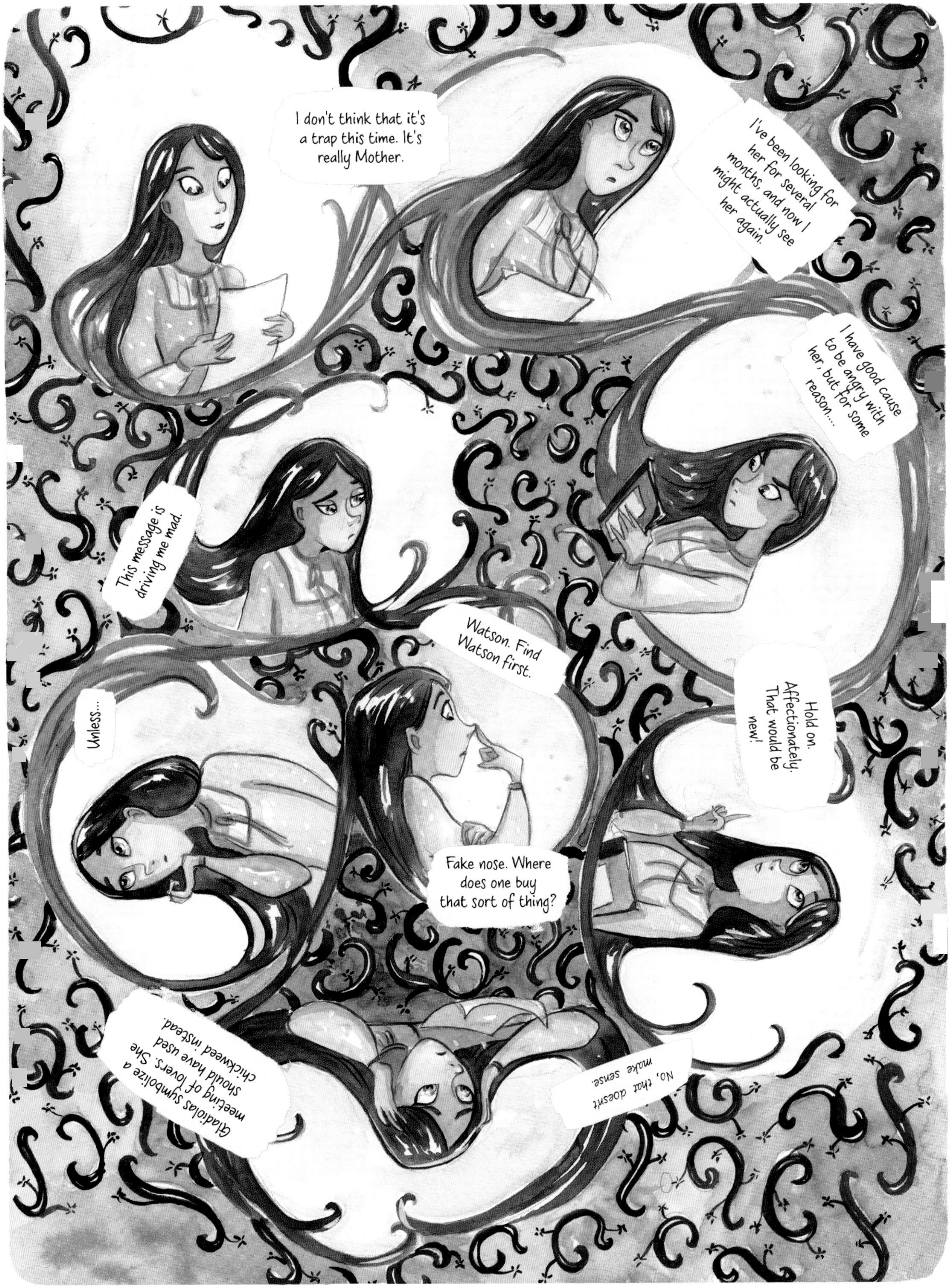
I don't think that it's a trap this time. It's really Mother.
I've been looking for her for several months, and now I might actually see her again.
I have good cause to be angry with her, but for some reason....
This message is driving me mad.
Watson. Find Watson first.
Hold on. Affectionately. That would be new!
Unless...
Fake nose. Where does one buy that sort of thing?
No, that doesn't make sense.
Gladiolias symbolize a meeting of lovers. She should have used chickweed instead.

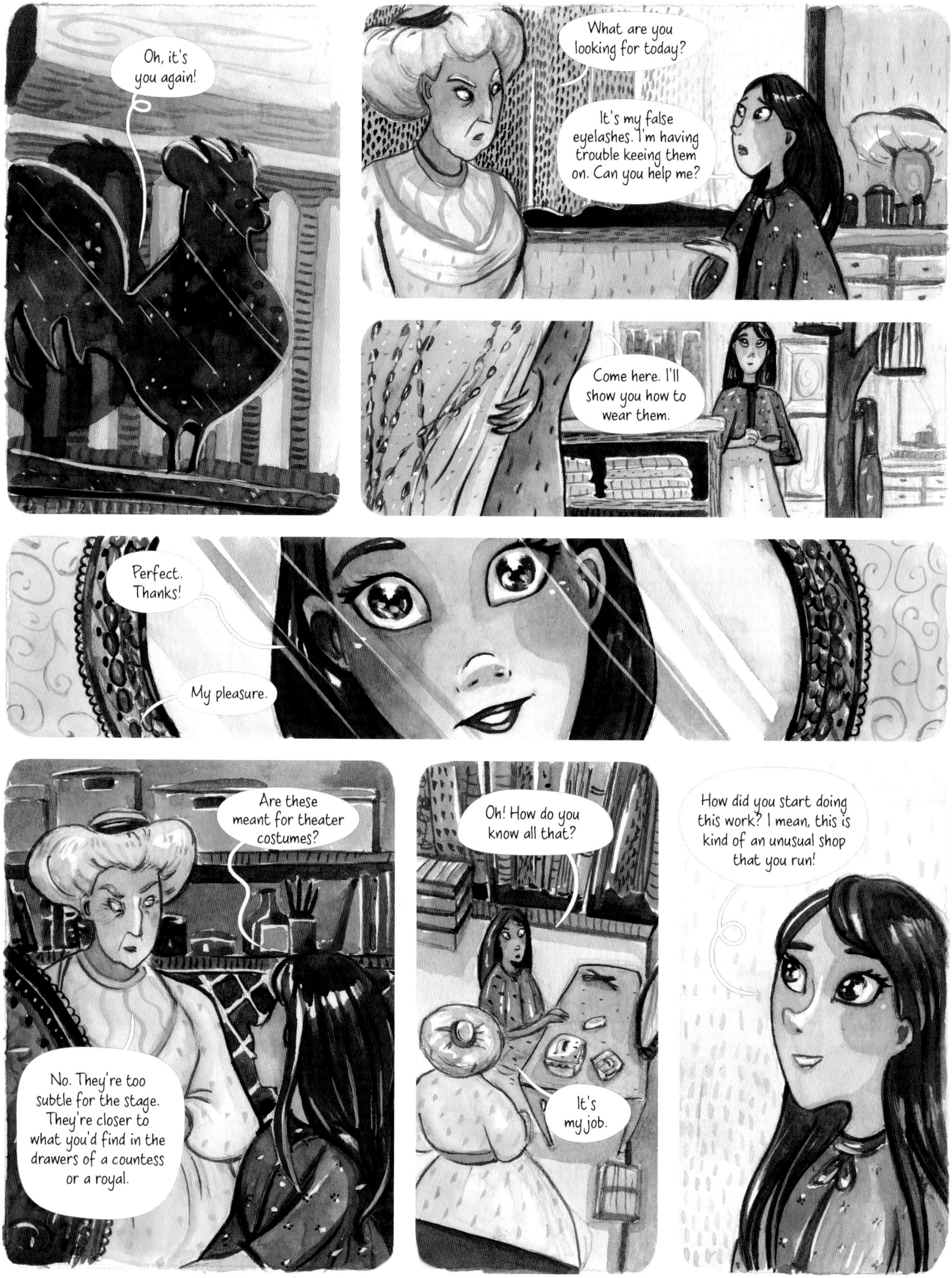

Oh, it's you again!
What are you looking for today?
It's my false eyelashes. I'm having trouble keeing them on. Can you help me?
Come here. I'll show you how to wear them.
Perfect. Thanks!
My pleasure.
Are these meant for theater costumes?
No. They're too subtle for the stage. They're closer to what you'd find in the drawers of a countess or a royal.
Oh! How do you know all that?
It's my job.
How did you start doing this work? I mean, this is kind of an unusual shop that you run!

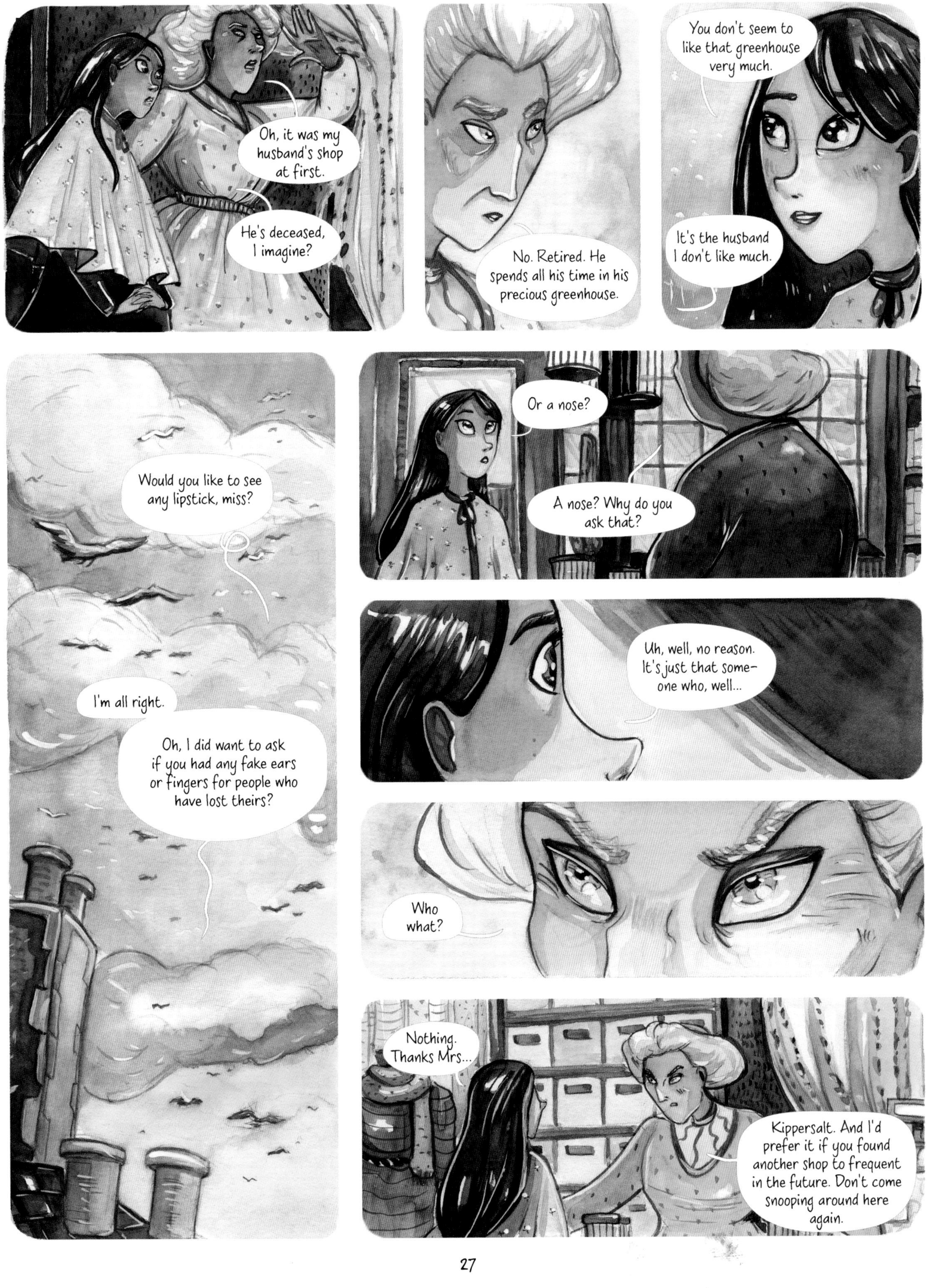
Oh, it was my husband's shop at first.
He's deceased, I imagine?
No. Retired. He spends all his time in his precious greenhouse.
You don't seem to like that greenhouse very much.
It's the husband I don't like much.
Would you like to see any lipstick, miss?
I'm all right.
Oh, I did want to ask if you had any fake ears or fingers for people who have lost theirs?
Or a nose?
A nose? Why do you ask that?
Uh, well, no reason. It's just that some-one who, well...
Who what?
Nothing. Thanks Mrs...
Kippersalt. And I'd prefer it if you found another shop to frequent in the future. Don't come snooping around here again.

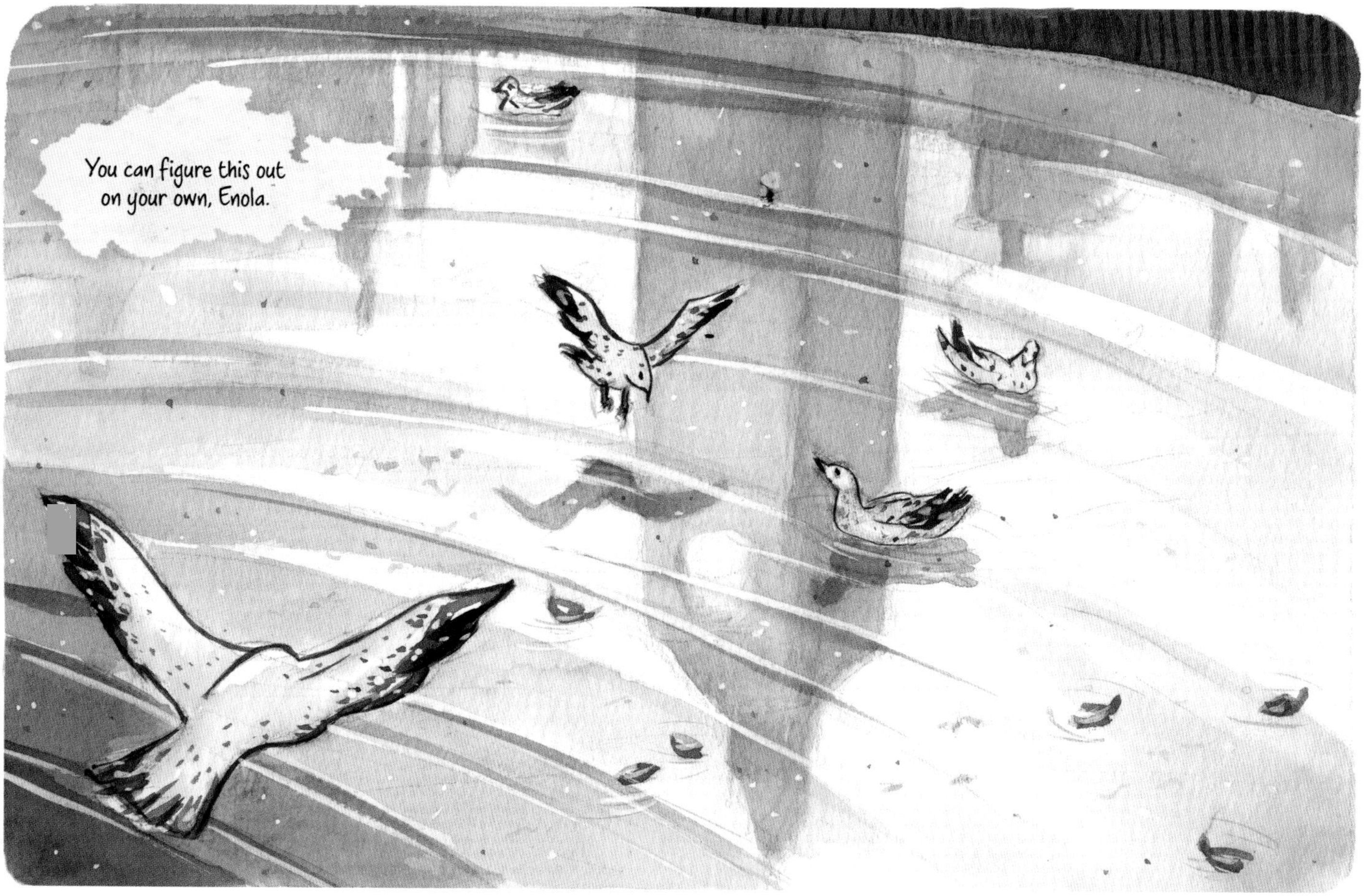
You can figure this out on your own, Enola.

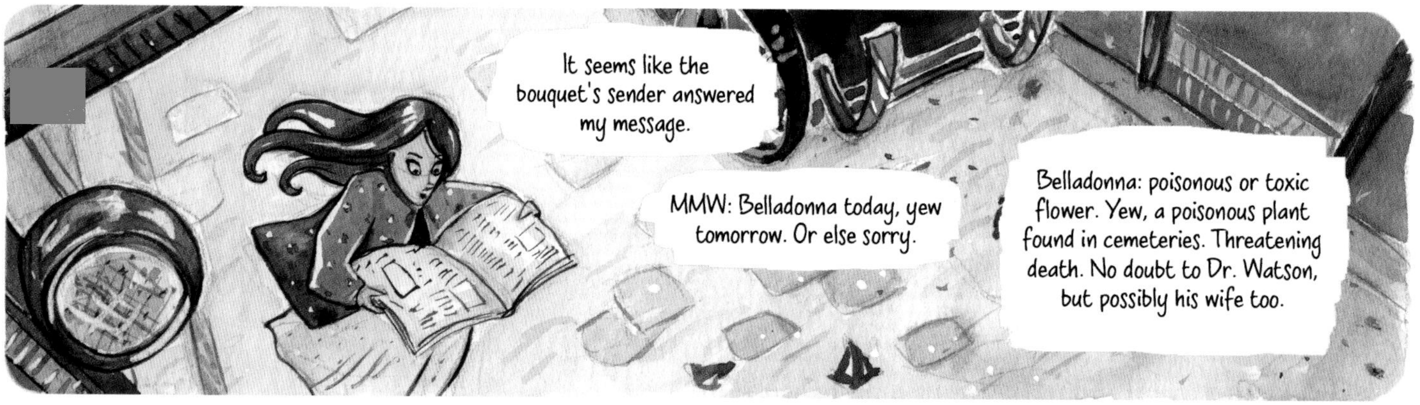
It seems like the bouquet's sender answered my message.
MMW: Belladonna today, yew tomorrow. Or else sorry.
Belladonna: poisonous or toxic flower. Yew, a poisonous plant found in cemeteries. Threatening death. No doubt to Dr. Watson, but possibly his wife too.

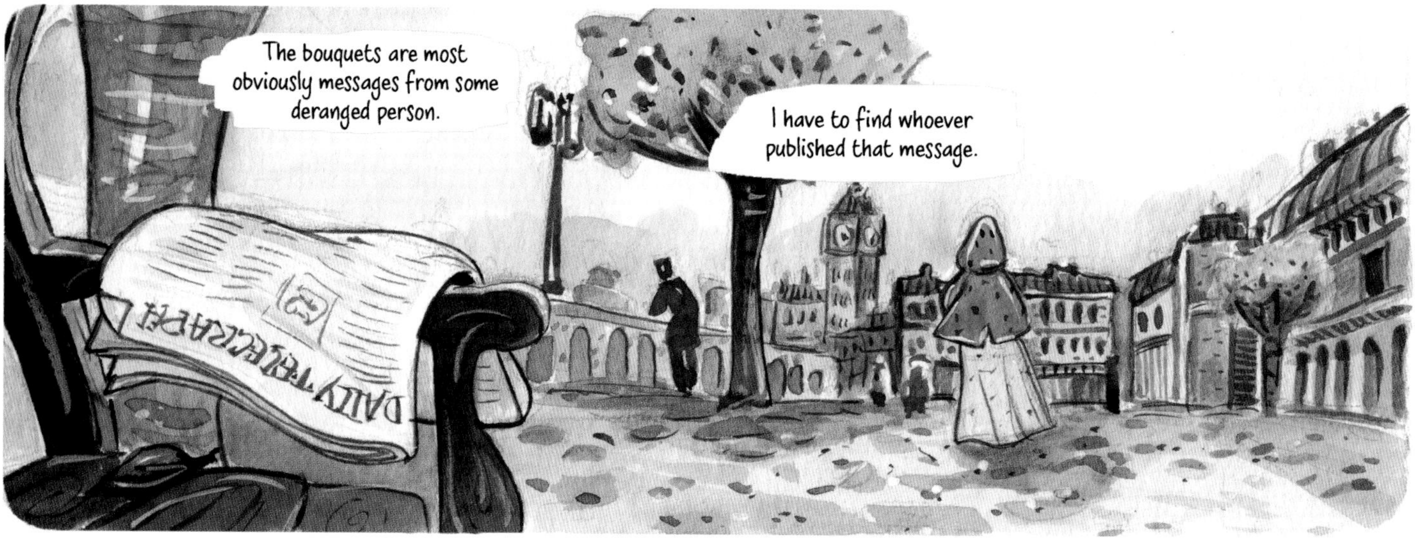
The bouquets are most obviously messages from some deranged person.
I have to find whoever published that message.

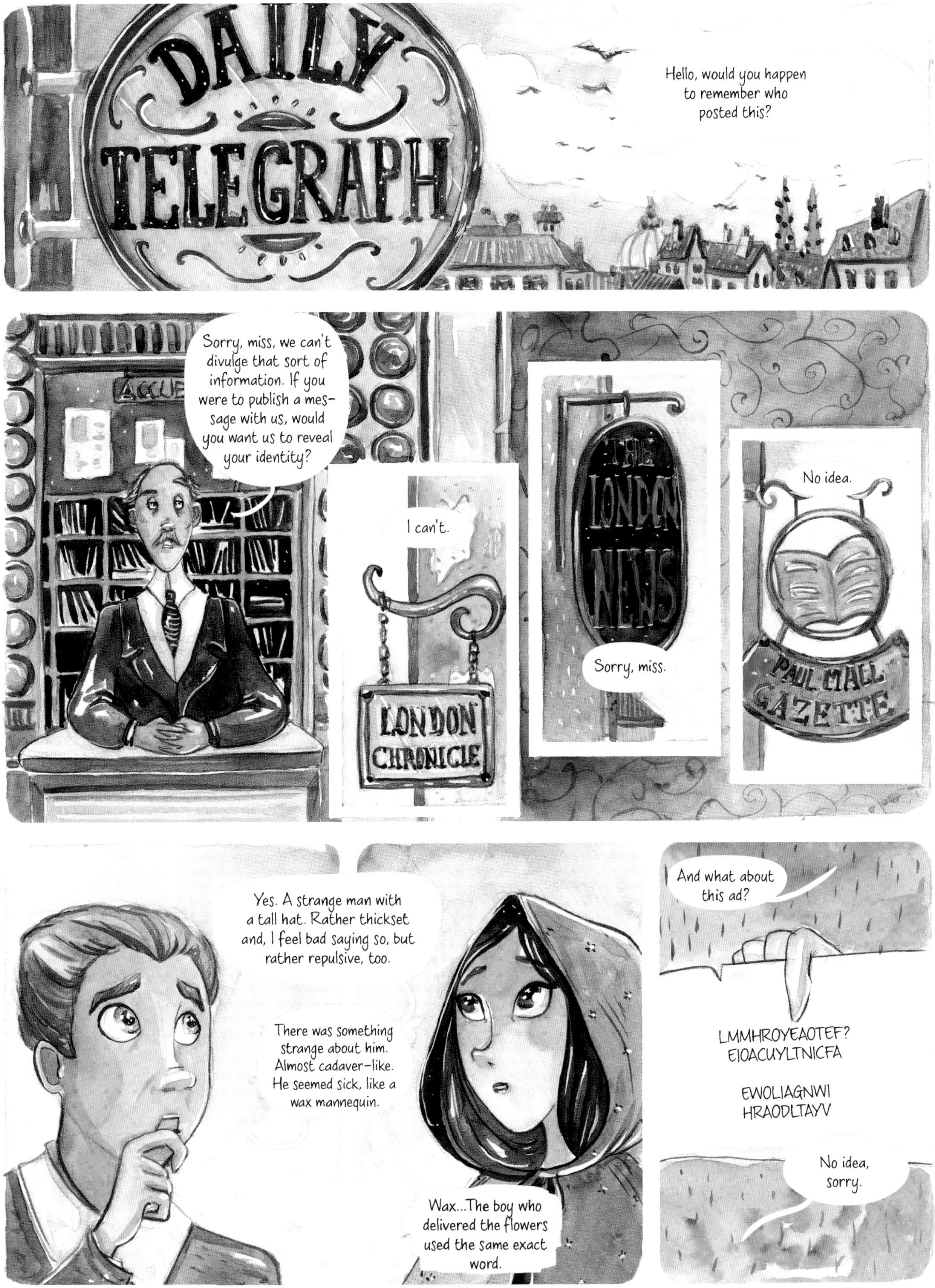
DAILY TELEGRAPH
Hello, would you happen to remember who posted this?
Sorry, miss, we can't divulge that sort of information. If you were to publish a message with us, would you want us to reveal your identity?
I can't.
LONDON CHRONICLE
THE LONDON NEWS
Sorry, miss.
No idea.
PAUL MALL GAZETTE
Yes. A strange man with a tall hat. Rather thickset and, I feel bad saying so, but rather repulsive, too.
There was something strange about him. Almost cadaver-like. He seemed sick, like a wax mannequin.
Wax...The boy who delivered the flowers used the same exact word.
And what about this ad?
LMMHROYEAOTEF? EIOACUYLTNICFA
EWOLIAGNWI HRAODLTAYV
No idea, sorry.

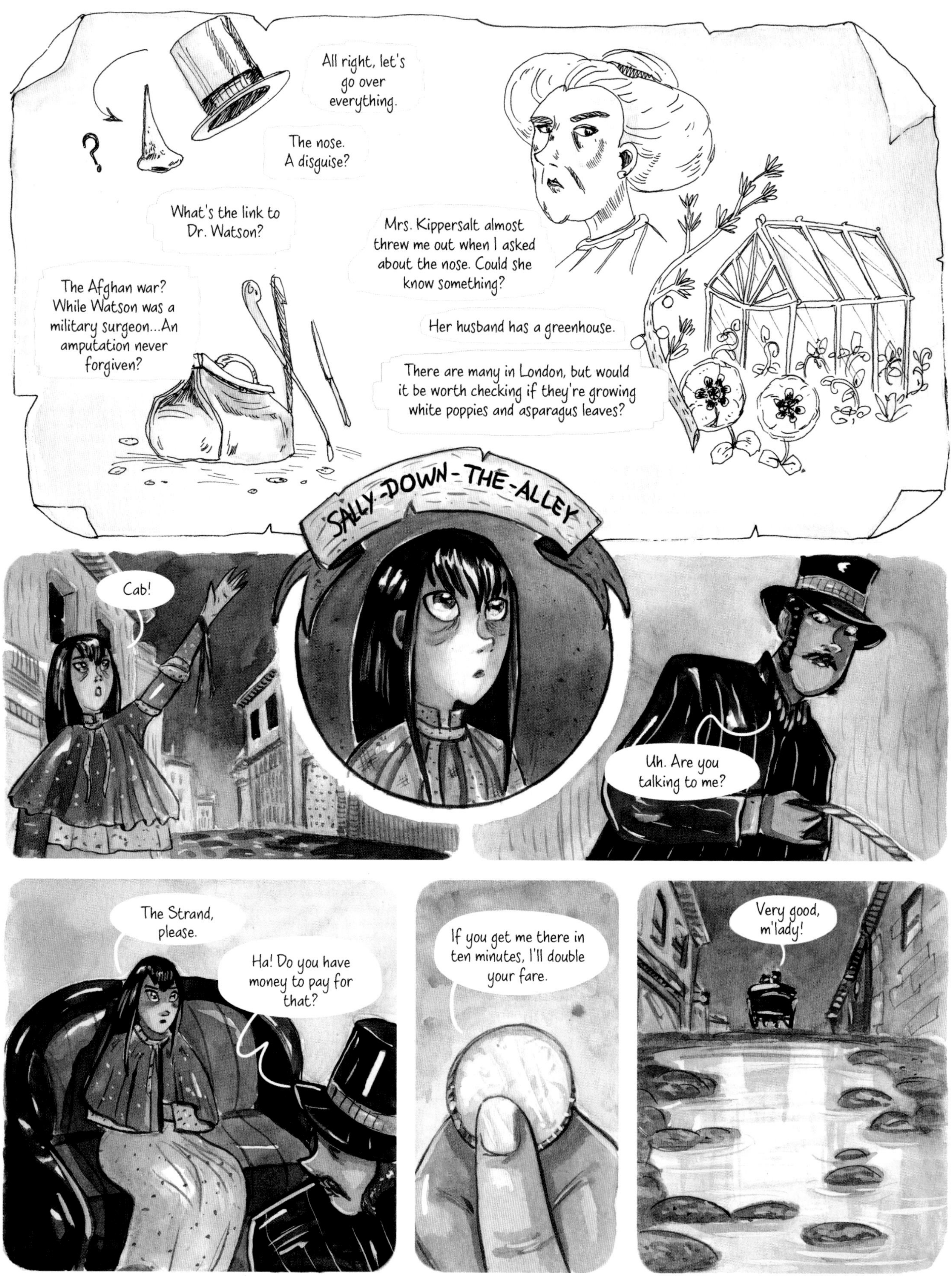
All right, let's go over everything.
The nose. A disguise?
What's the link to Dr. Watson?
The Afghan war? While Watson was a military surgeon...An amputation never forgiven?
Mrs. Kippersalt almost threw me out when I asked about the nose. Could she know something?
Her husband has a greenhouse.
There are many in London, but would it be worth checking if they're growing white poppies and asparagus leaves?
SALLY-DOWN-THE-ALLEY
Cab!
Uh. Are you talking to me?
The Strand, please.
Ha! Do you have money to pay for that?
If you get me there in ten minutes, I'll double your fare.
Very good, m'lady!

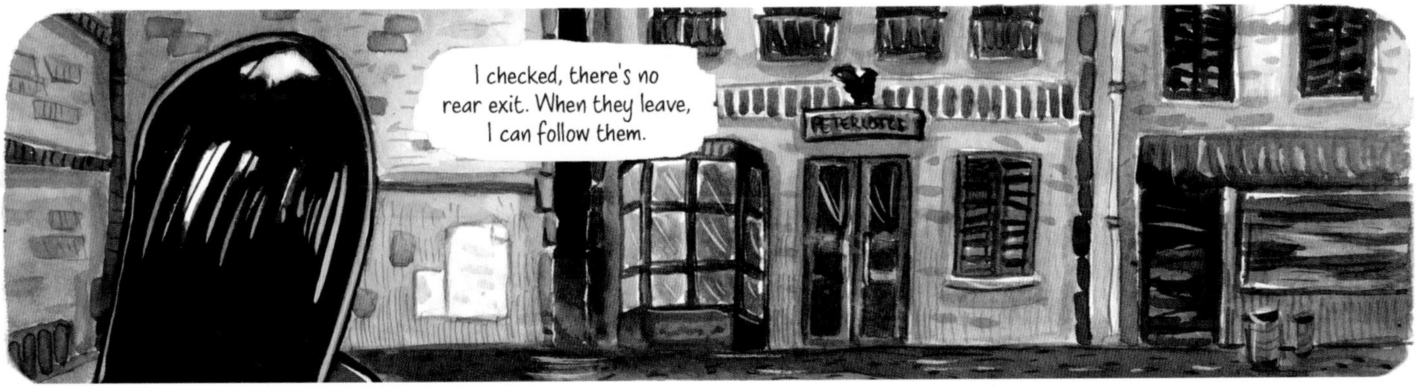
I checked, there's no rear exit. When they leave, I can follow them.

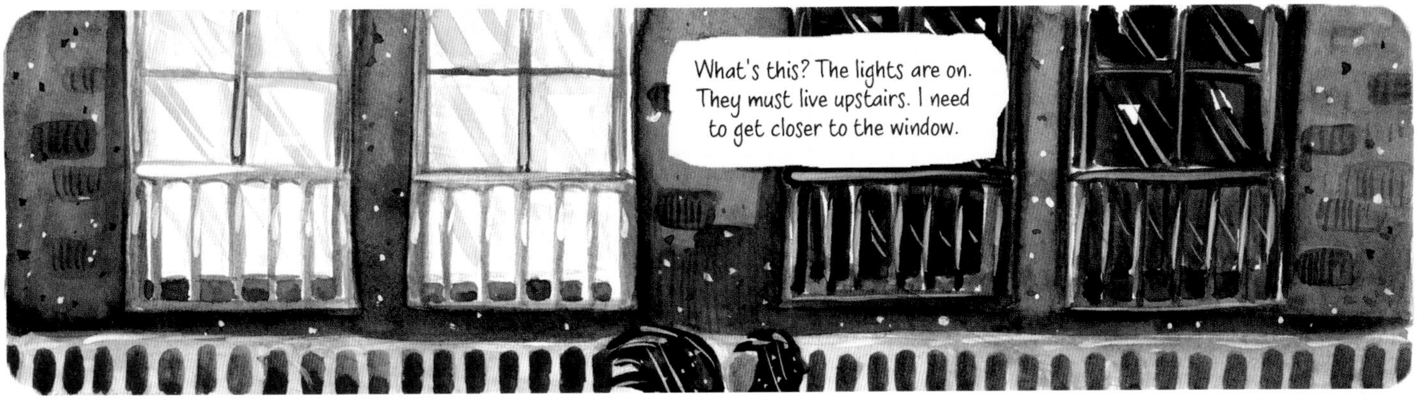
What's this? The lights are on. They must live upstairs. I need to get closer to the window.

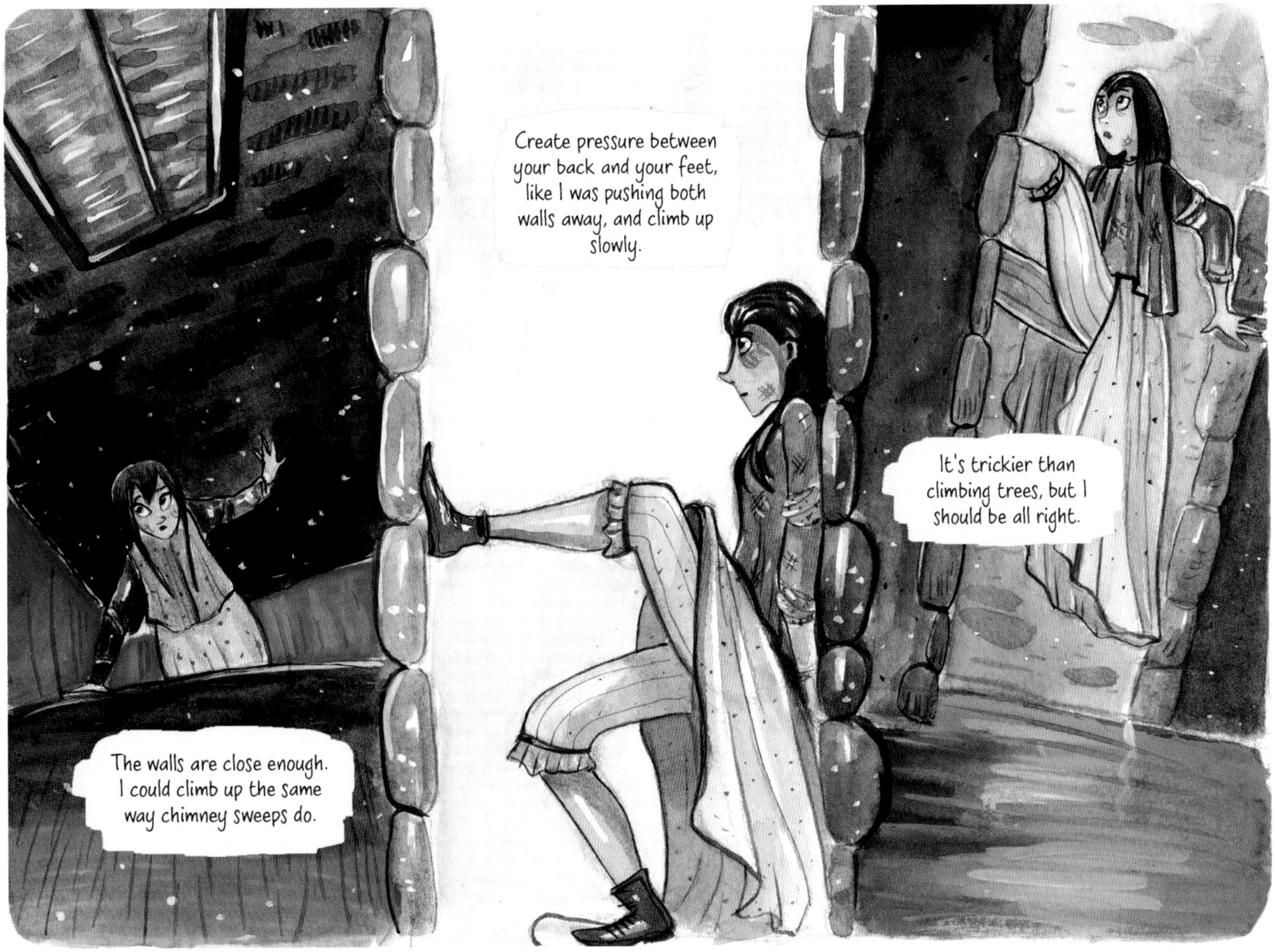
The walls are close enough. I could climb up the same way chimney sweeps do.
Create pressure between your back and your feet, like I was pushing both walls away, and climb up slowly.
It's trickier than climbing trees, but I should be all right.

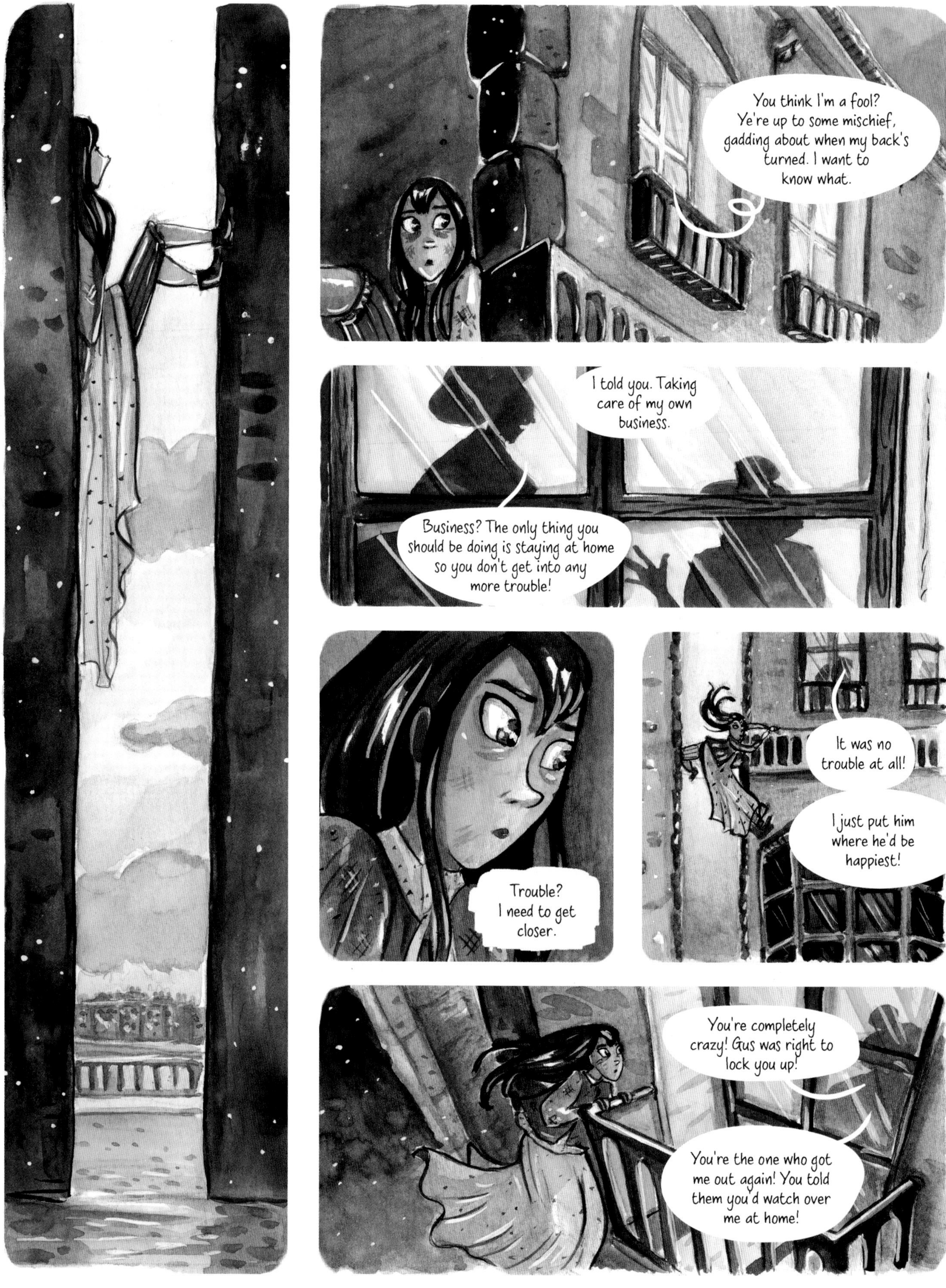
You think I'm a fool? Ye're up to some mischief, gadding about when my back's turned. I want to know what.
I told you. Taking care of my own business.
Business? The only thing you should be doing is staying at home so you don't get into any more trouble!
Trouble? I need to get closer.
It was no trouble at all!
I just put him where he'd be happiest!
You're completely crazy! Gus was right to lock you up!
You're the one who got me out again! You told them you'd watch over me at home!

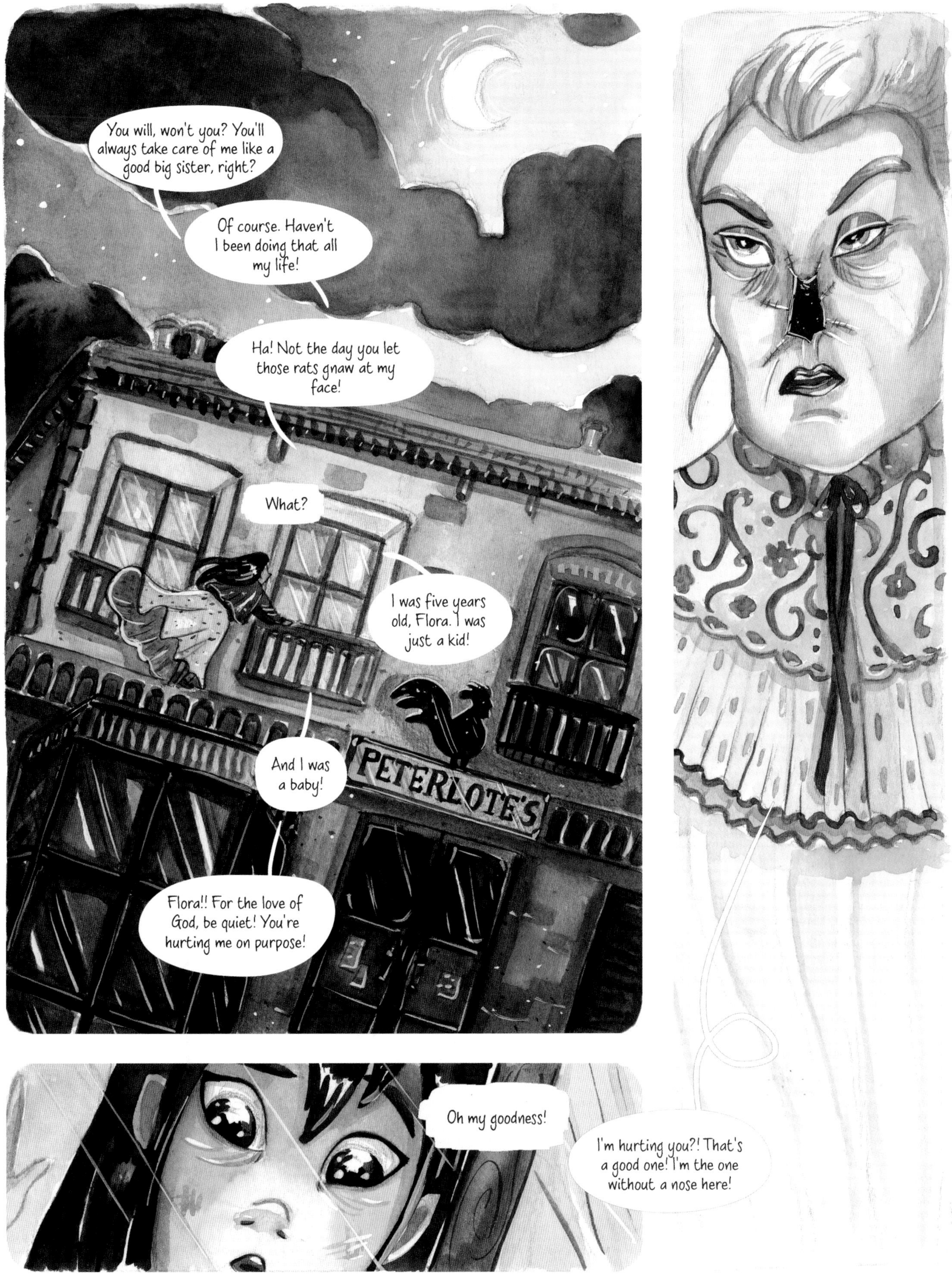
You will, won't you? You'll always take care of me like a good big sister, right?
Of course. Haven't I been doing that all my life!
Ha! Not the day you let those rats gnaw at my face!
What?
I was five years old, Flora. I was just a kid!
And I was a baby!
PETERLOTE'S
Flora!! For the love of God, be quiet! You're hurting me on purpose!
Oh my goodness!
I'm hurting you?! That's a good one! I'm the one without a nose here!

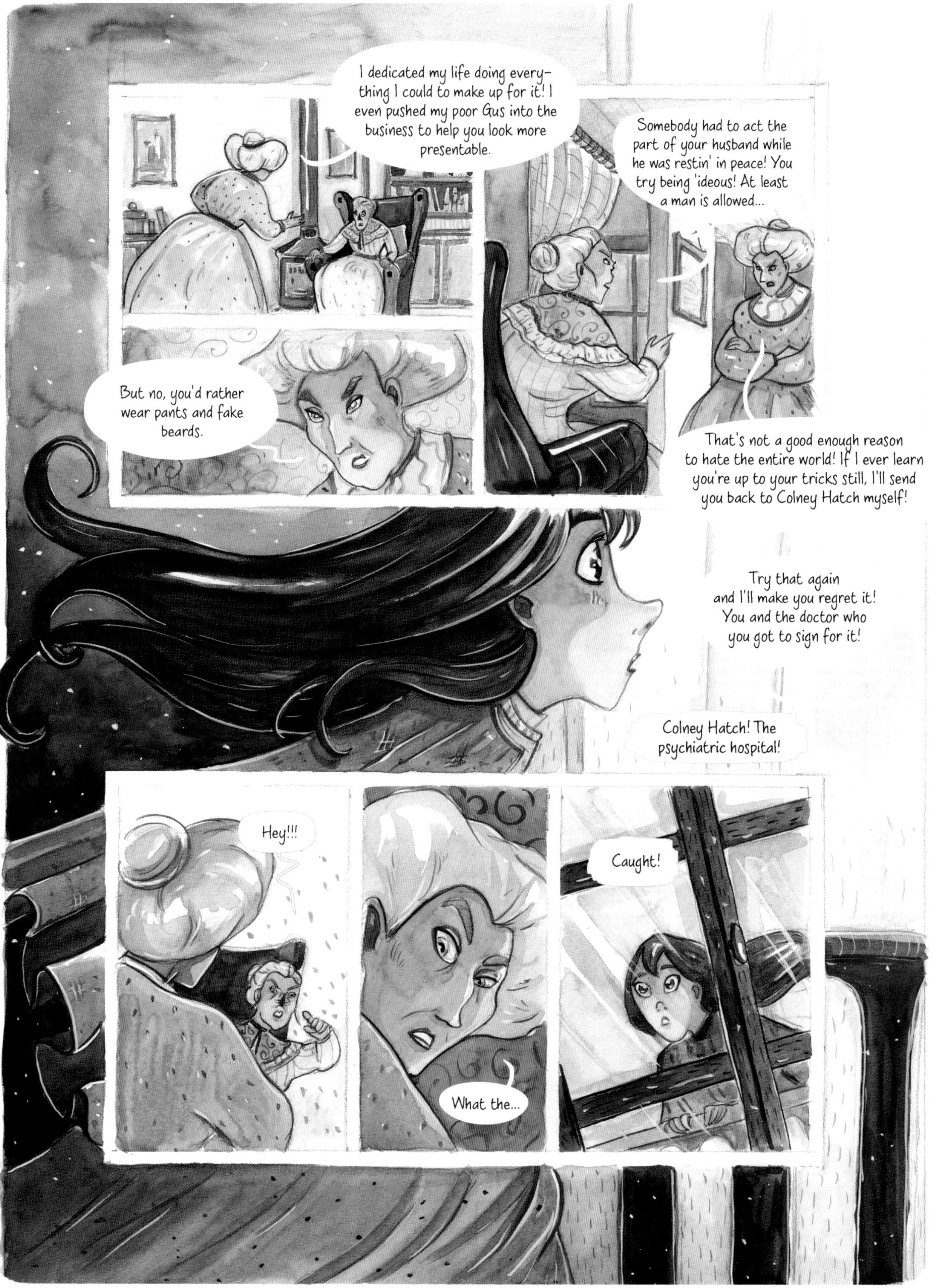
I dedicated my life doing everything I could to make up for it! I even pushed my poor Gus into the business to help you look more presentable.
But no, you'd rather wear pants and fake beards.
Somebody had to act the part of your husband while he was restin' in peace! You try being 'ideous! At least a man is allowed...
That's not a good enough reason to hate the entire world! If I ever learn you're up to your tricks still, I'll send you back to Colney Hatch myself!
Try that again and I'll make you regret it! You and the doctor who you got to sign for it!
Colney Hatch! The psychiatric hospital!
Hey!!!
What the...
Caught!

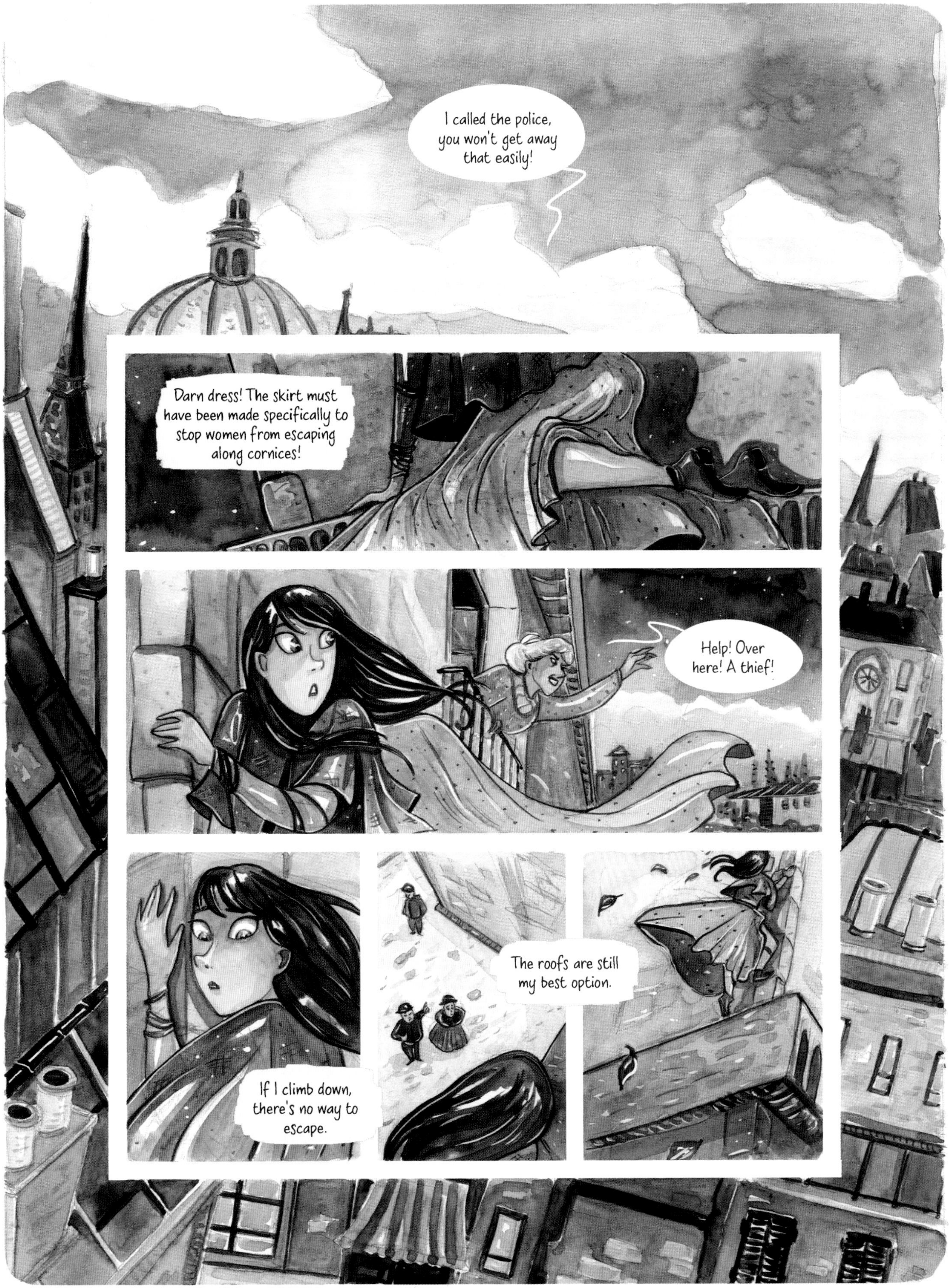
I called the police, you won't get away that easily!
Darn dress! The skirt must have been made specifically to stop women from escaping along cornices!
Help! Over here! A thief!
If I climb down, there's no way to escape.
The roofs are still my best option.

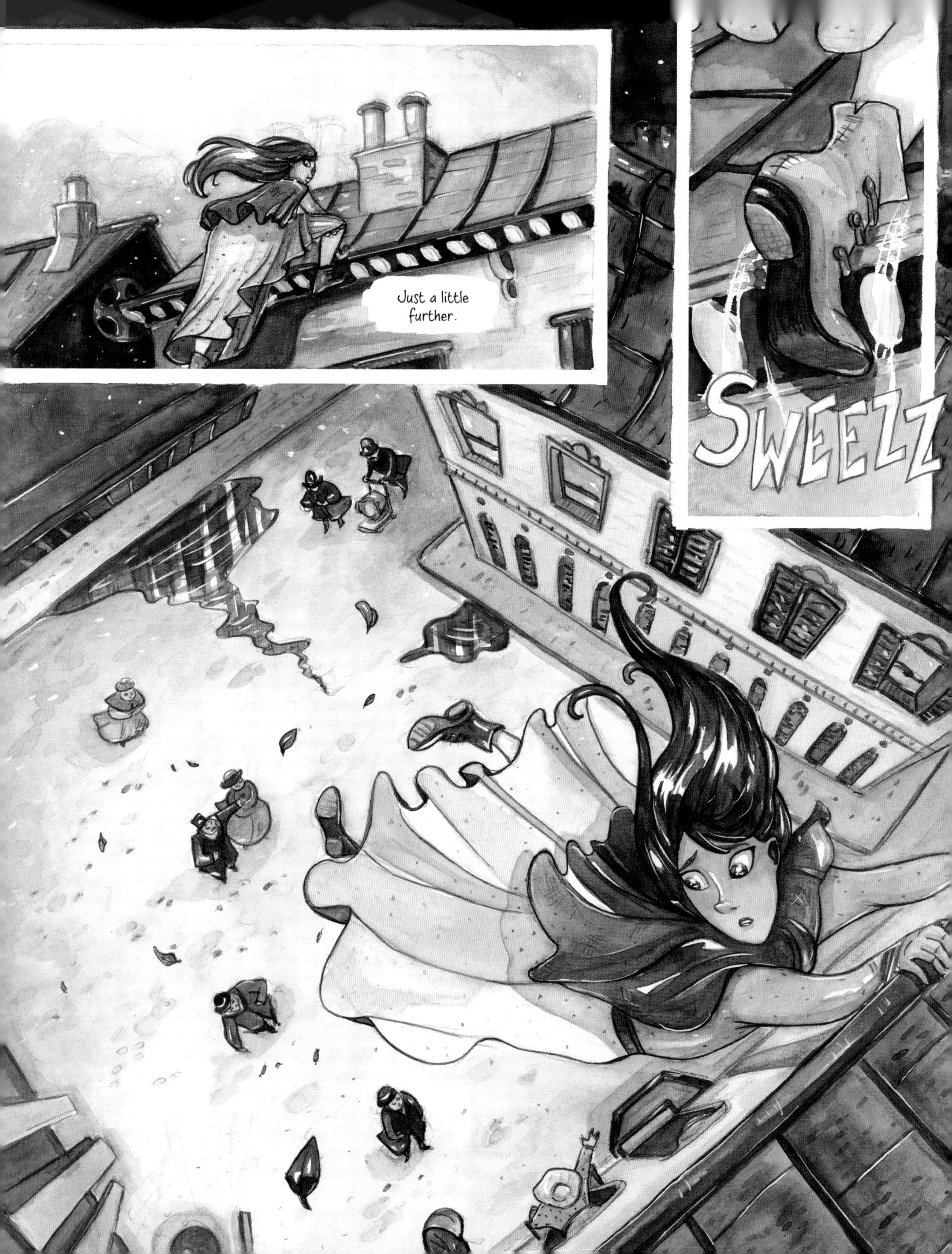
Just a little further.
SWEEZZ

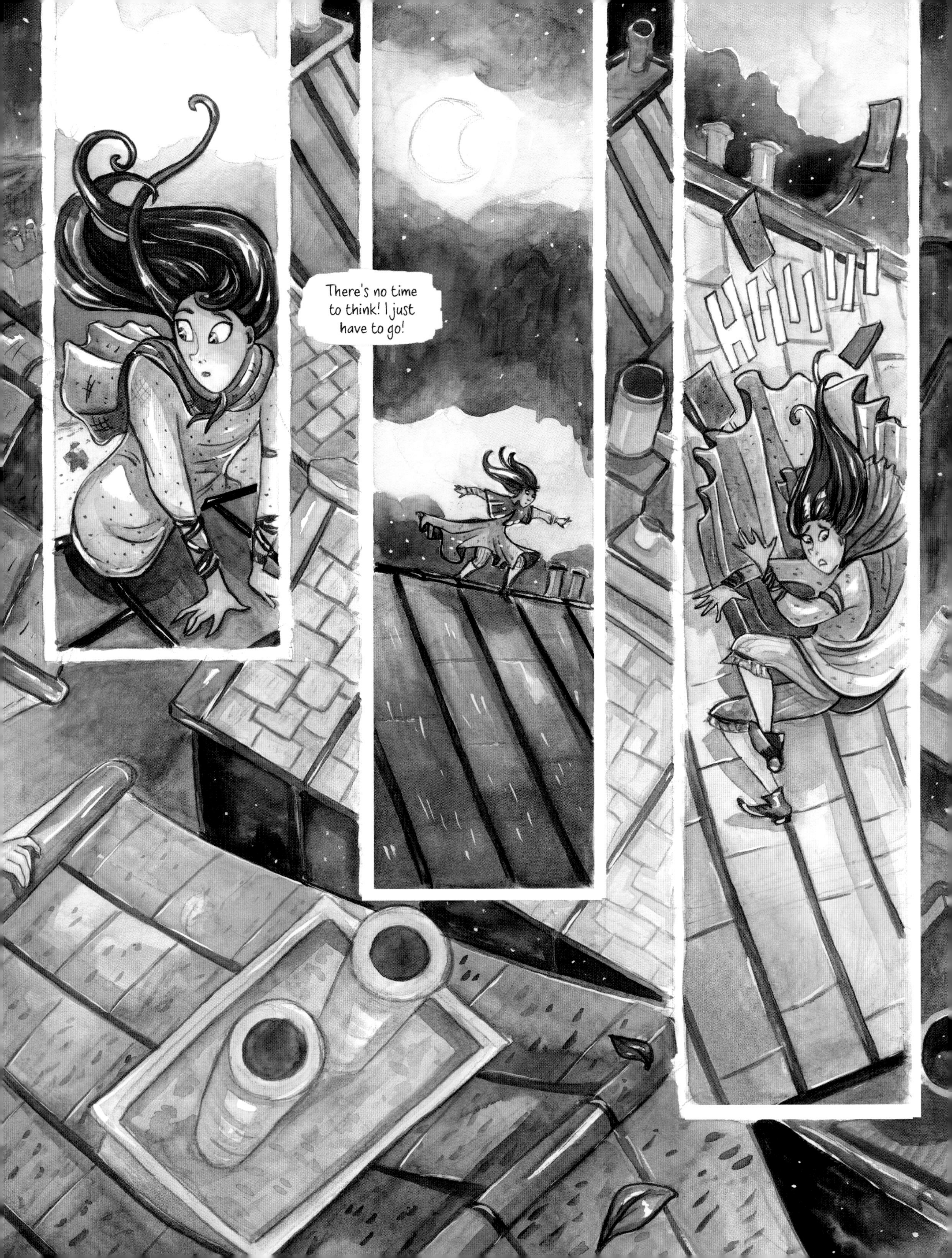
There's no time to think! I just have to go!

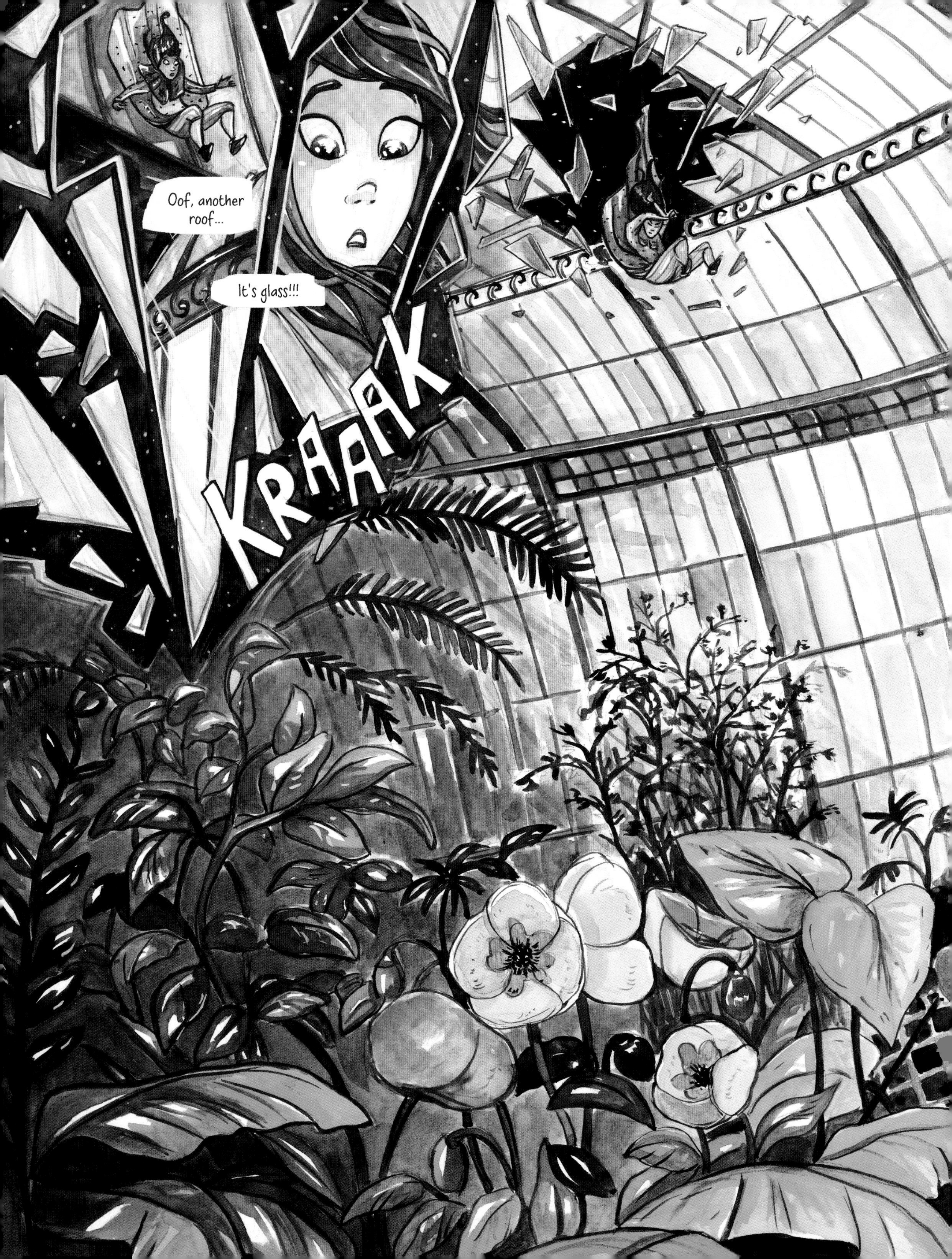
Oof, another roof...
It's glass!!!
KRAAAK

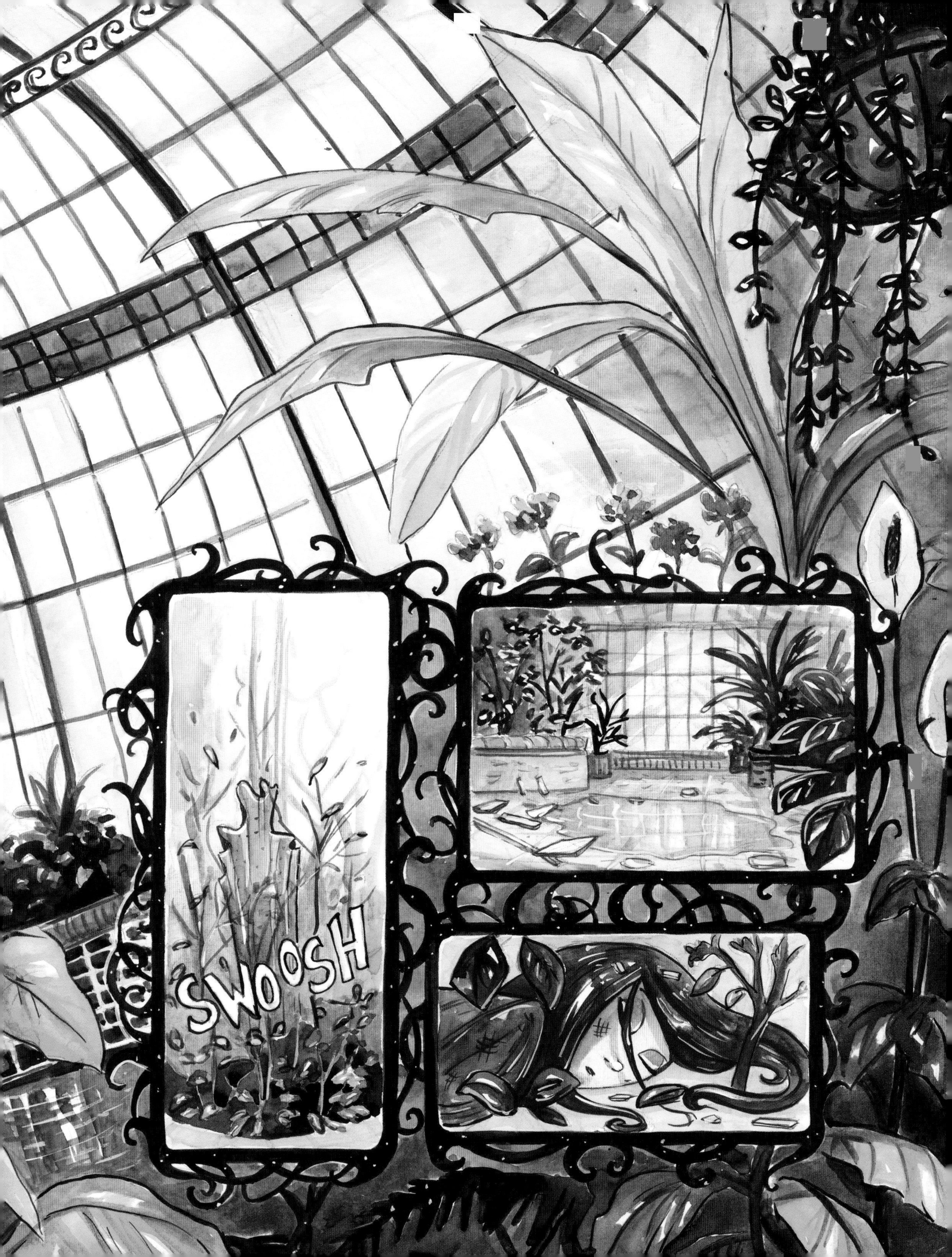
SWOOSH

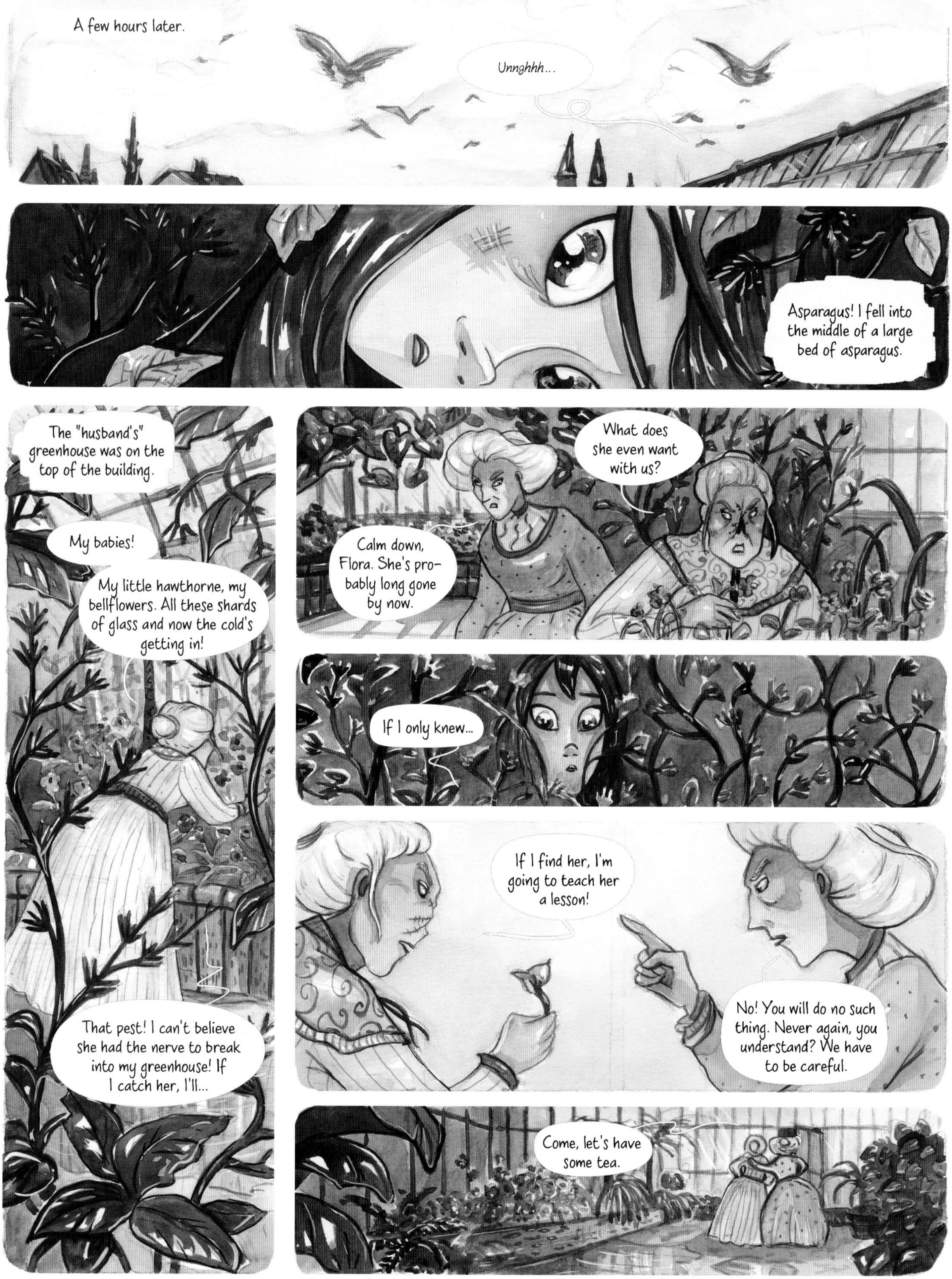
A few hours later.
Unnghhh...
Asparagus! I fell into the middle of a large bed of asparagus.
The "husband's" greenhouse was on the top of the building.
My babies!
My little hawthorne, my bellflowers. All these shards of glass and now the cold's getting in!
That pest! I can't believe she had the nerve to break into my greenhouse! If I catch her, I'll...
What does she even want with us?
Calm down, Flora. She's probably long gone by now.
If I only knew...
If I find her, I'm going to teach her a lesson!
No! You will do no such thing. Never again, you understand? We have to be careful.
Come, let's have some tea.

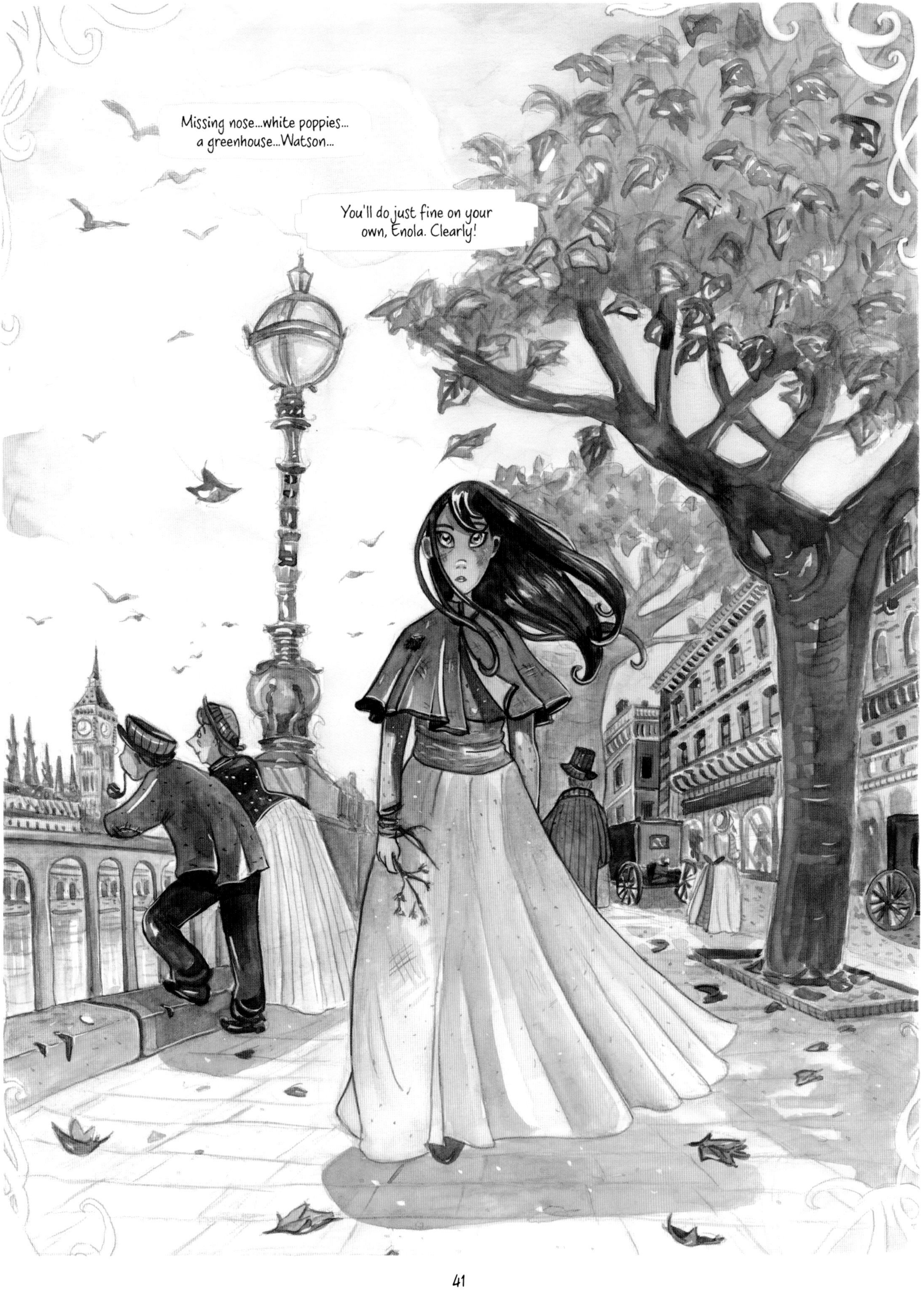
Missing nose...white poppies... a greenhouse...Watson...
You'll do just fine on your own, Enola. Clearly!

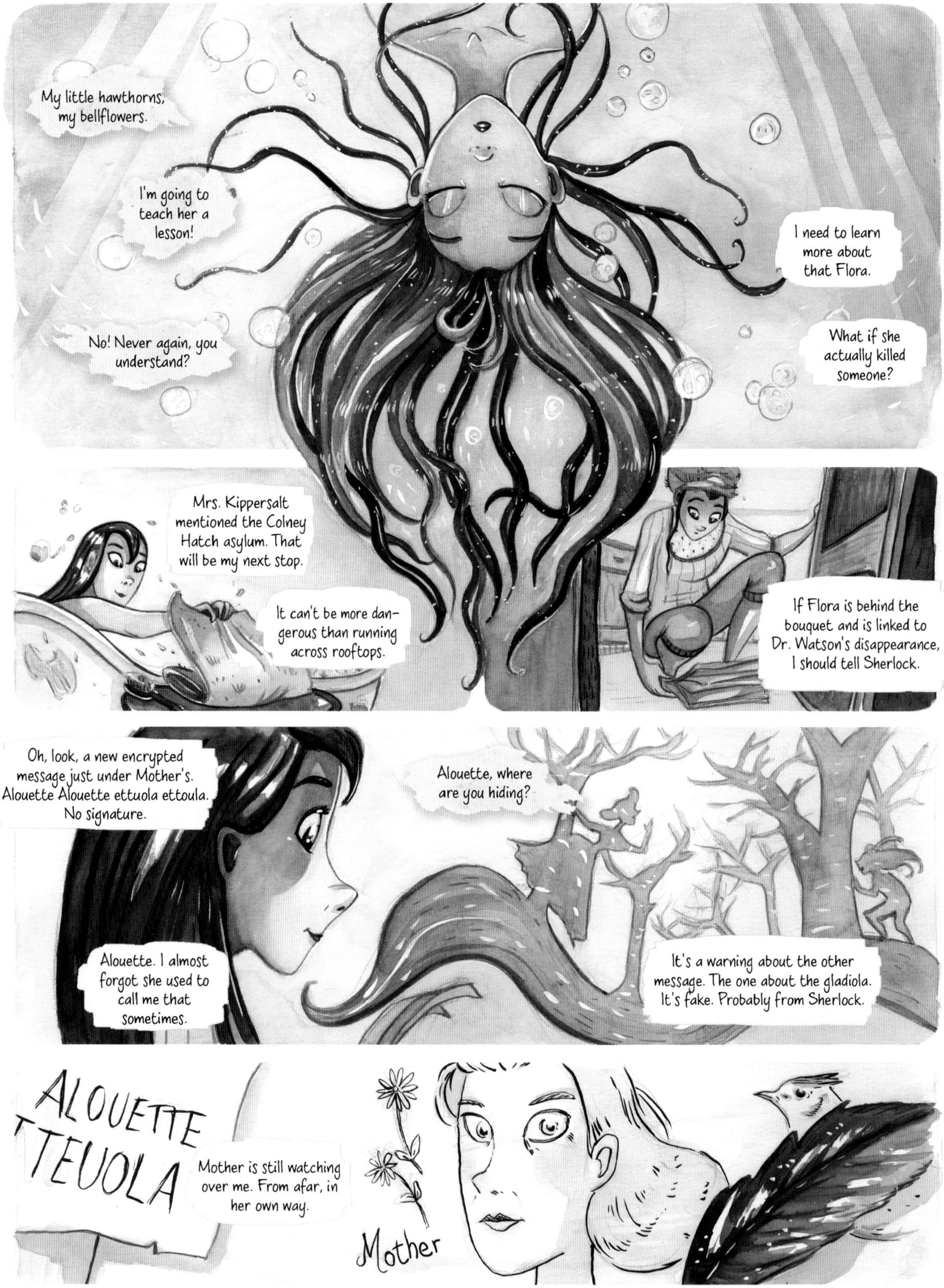
My little hawthorns, my bellflowers.
I'm going to teach her a lesson!
No! Never again, you understand?
I need to learn more about that Flora.
What if she actually killed someone?
Mrs. Kippersalt mentioned the Colney Hatch asylum. That will be my next stop.
It can't be more dangerous than running across rooftops.
If Flora is behind the bouquet and is linked to Dr. Watson's disappearance, I should tell Sherlock.
Oh, look, a new encrypted message just under Mother's. Alouette Alouette ettuola ettoula. No signature.
Alouette, where are you hiding?
Aloutte. I almost forgot she used to call me that sometimes.
It's a warning about the other message. The one about the gladiola. It's fake. Probably from Sherlock.
ALOUETTE
TTEUOLA
Mother is still watching over me. From afar, in her own way.
Mother

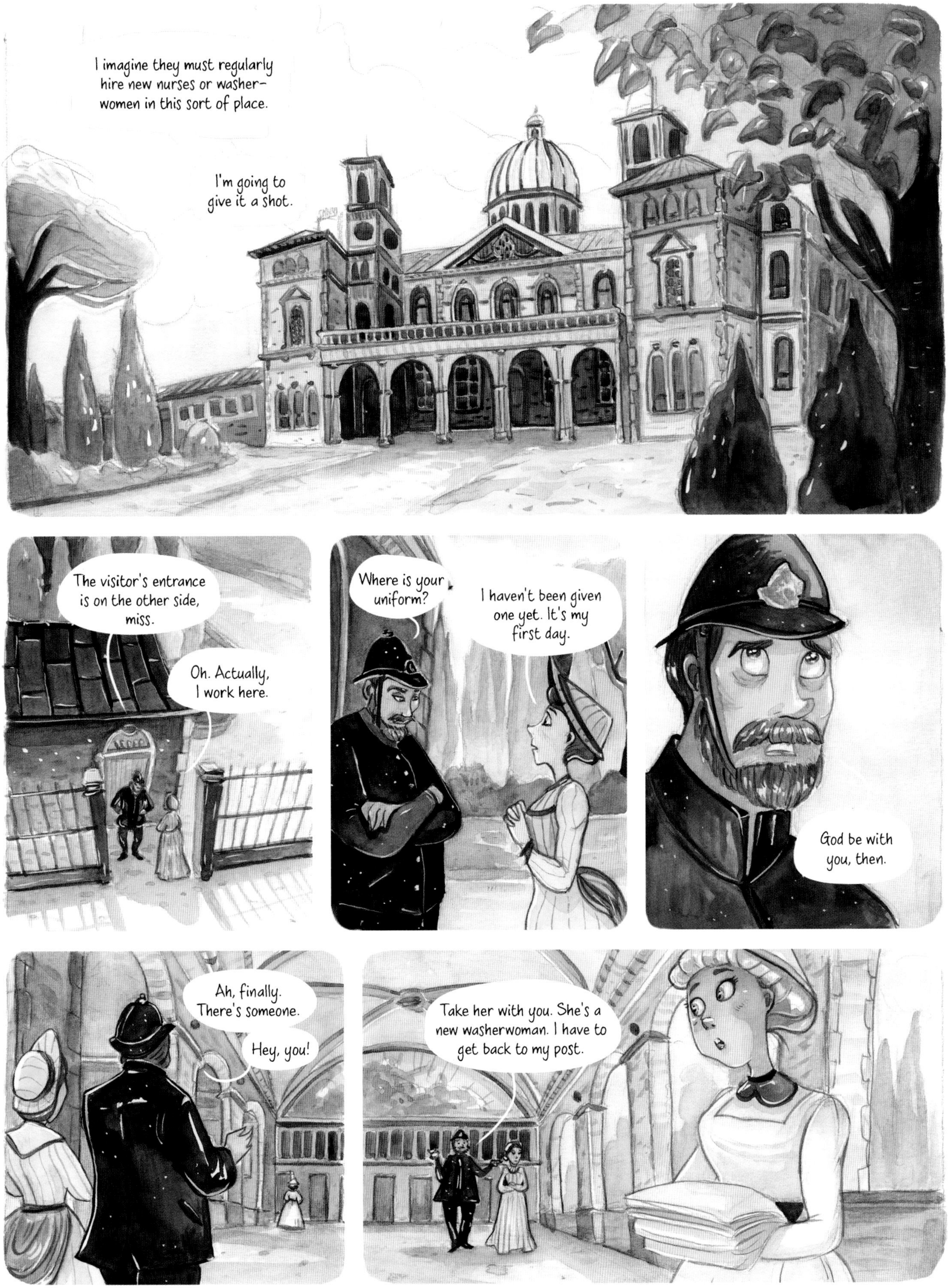
I imagine they must regularly hire new nurses or washer-women in this sort of place.
I'm going to give it a shot.
The visitor's entrance is on the other side, miss.
Oh. Actually, I work here.
Where is your uniform?
I haven't been given one yet. It's my first day.
God be with you, then.
Ah, finally. There's someone.
Hey, you!
Take her with you. She's a new washerwoman. I have to get back to my post.

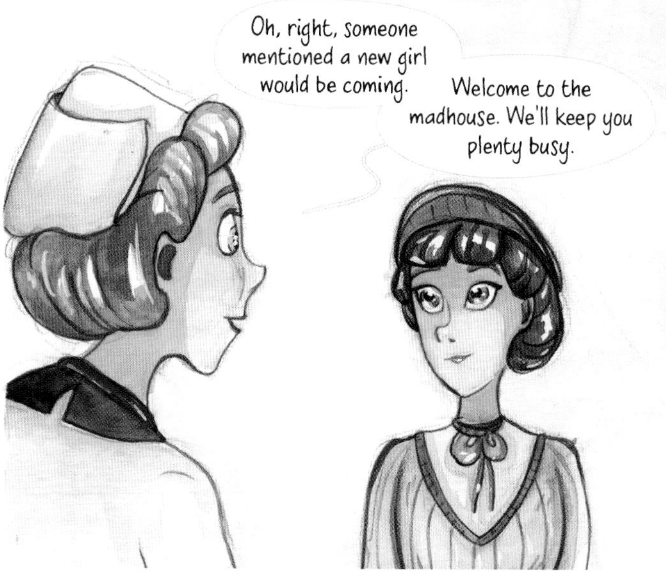
Oh, right, someone mentioned a new girl would be coming.
Welcome to the madhouse. We'll keep you plenty busy.

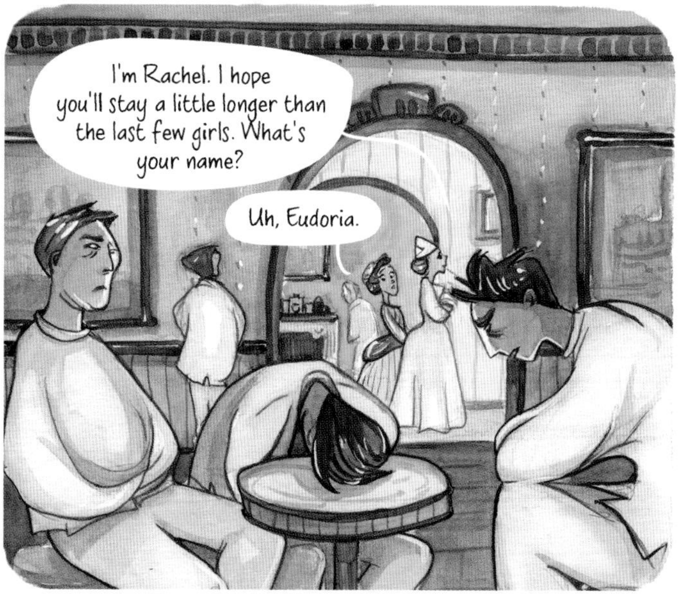
I'm Rachel. I hope you'll stay a little longer than the last few girls. What's your name?
Uh, Eudoria.

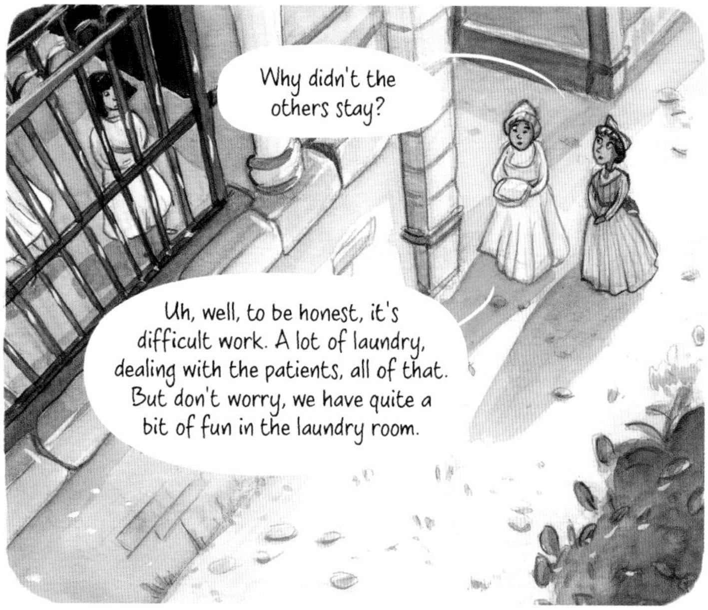
Why didn't the others stay?
Uh, well, to be honest, it's difficult work. A lot of laundry, dealing with the patients, all of that. But don't worry, we have quite a bit of fun in the laundry room.

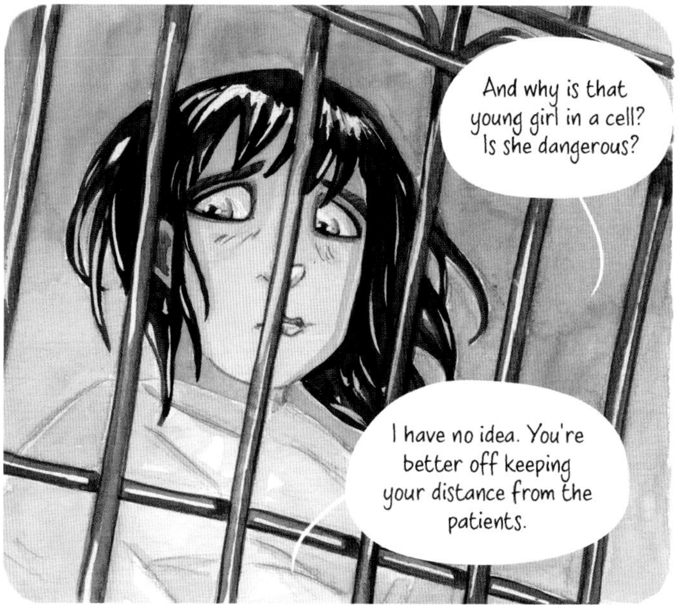
And why is that young girl in a cell? Is she dangerous?
I have no idea. You're better off keeping your distance from the patients.

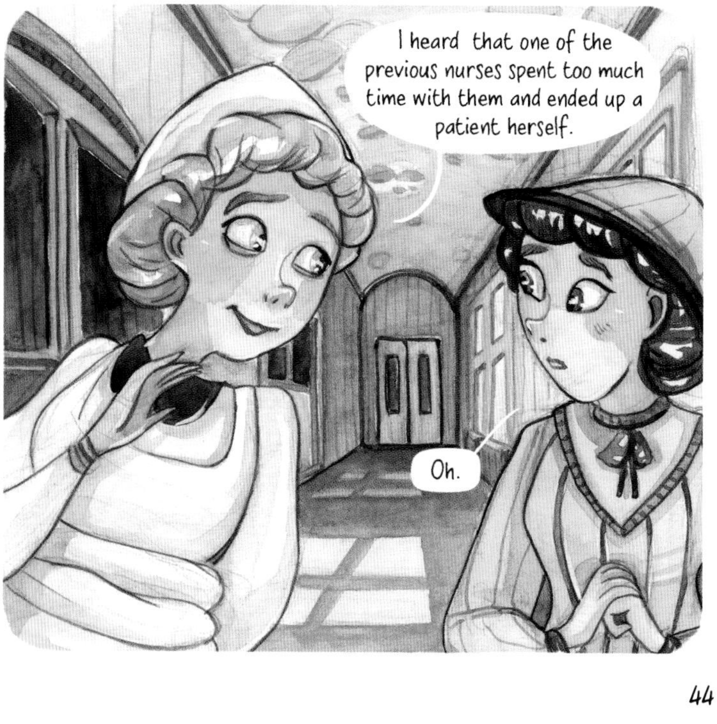
I heard that one of the previous nurses spent too much time with them and ended up a patient herself.
Oh.

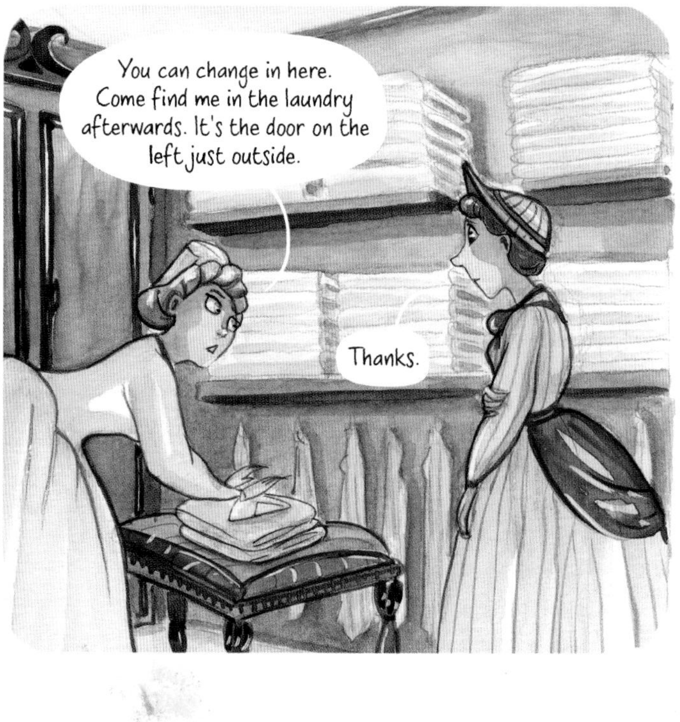
You can change in here. Come find me in the laundry afterwards. It's the door on the left just outside.
Thanks.

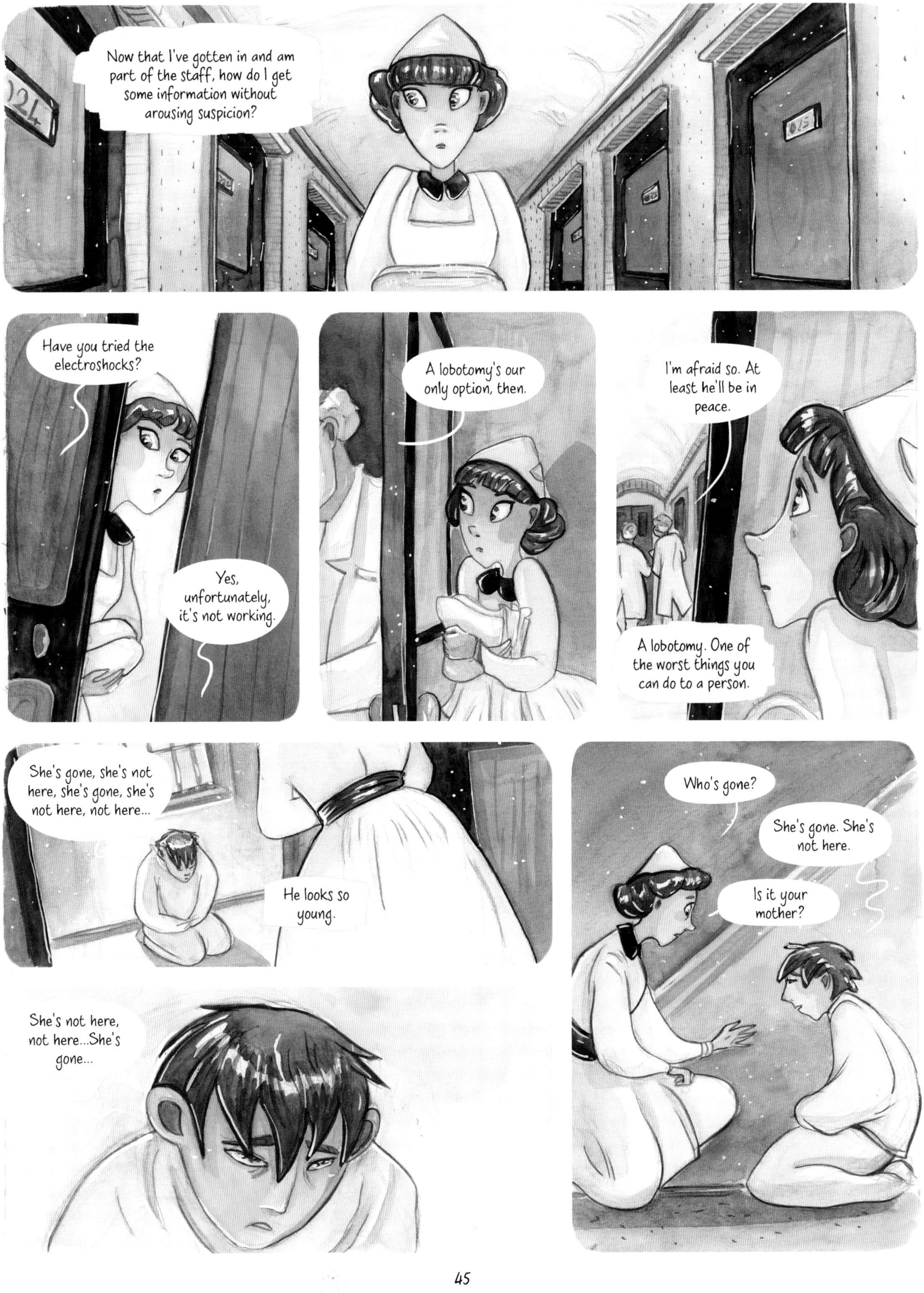
Now that I've gotten in and am part of the staff, how do I get some information without arousing suspicion?
Have you tried the electroshocks?
Yes, unfortunately, it's not working.
A lobotomy's our only option, then.
I'm afraid so. At least he'll be in peace.
A lobotomy. One of the worst things you can do to a person.
She's gone, she's not here, she's gone, she's not here, not here...
He looks so young.
She's not here, not here...She's gone...
Who's gone?
She's gone. She's not here.
Is it your mother?

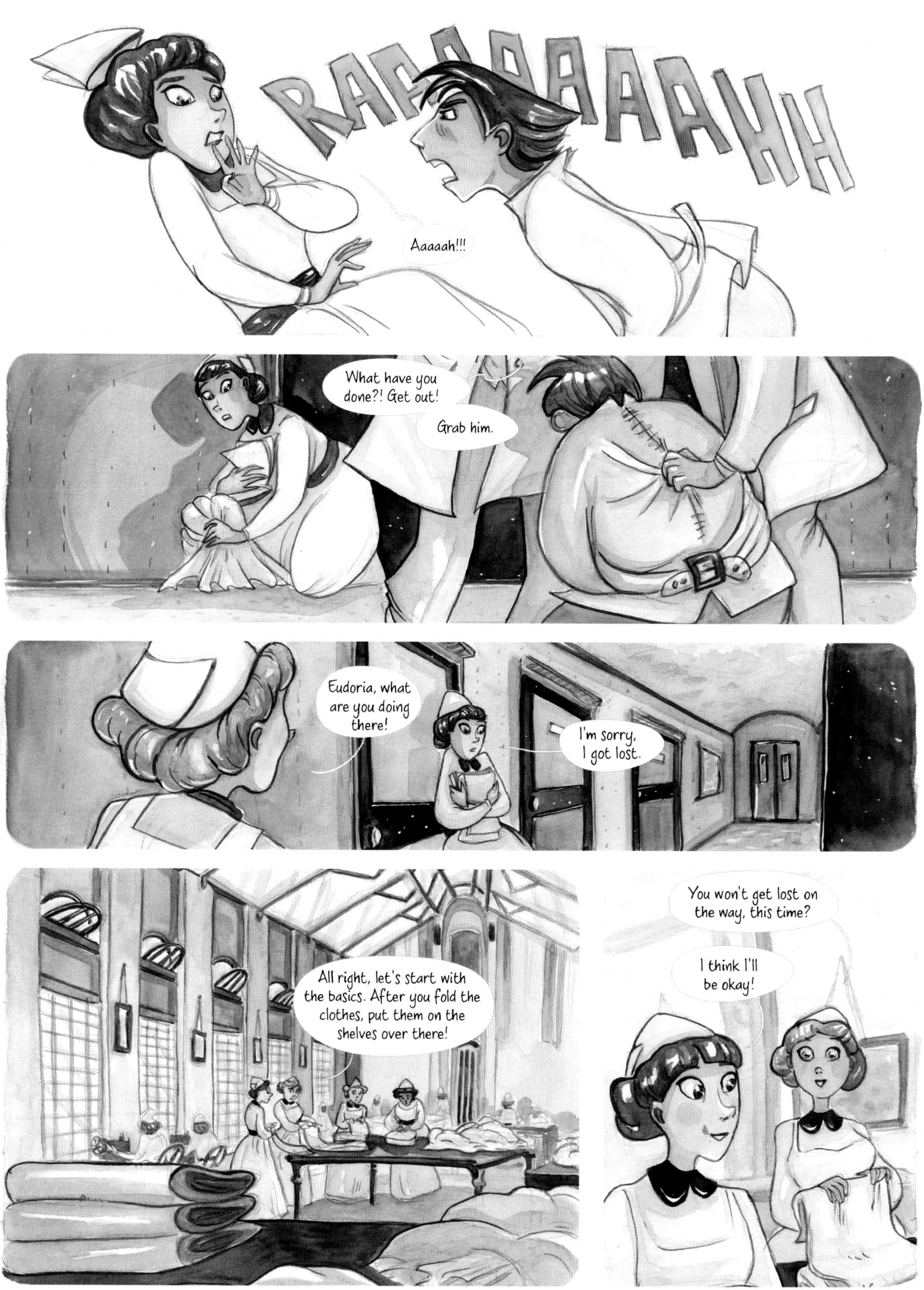
RAAAAAAAHH
Aaaaah!!!
What have you done?! Get out!
Grab him.
Eudoria, what are you doing there!
I'm sorry, I got lost.
All right, let's start with the basics. After you fold the clothes, put them on the shelves over there!
You won't get lost on the way, this time?
I think I'll be okay!

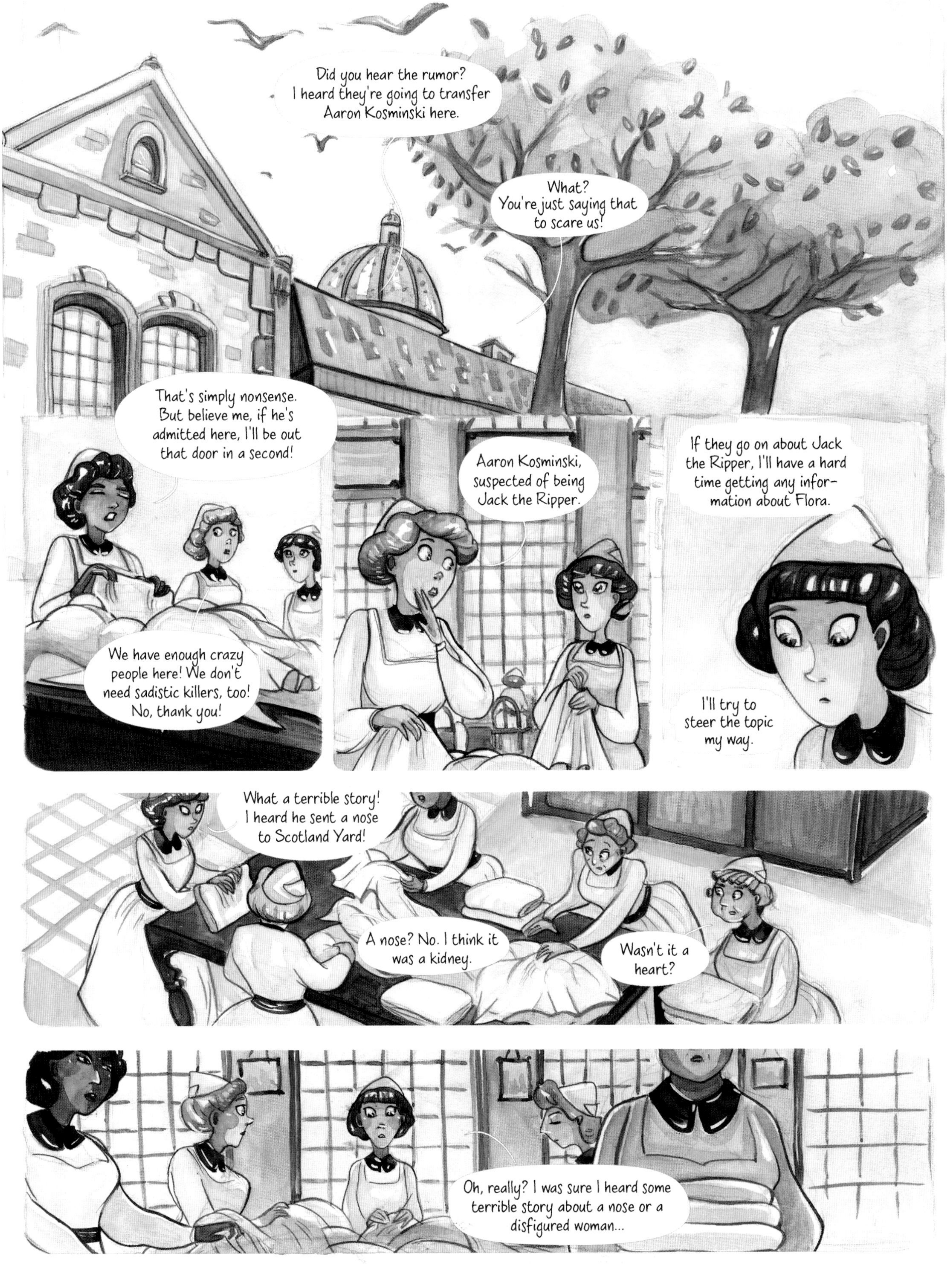
Did you hear the rumor? I heard they're going to transfer Aaron Kosminski here.
What? You're just saying that to scare us!
That's simply nonsense. But believe me, if he's admitted here, I'll be out that door in a second!
We have enough crazy people here! We don't need sadistic killers, too! No, thank you!
Aaron Kosminski, suspected of being Jack the Ripper.
If they go on about Jack the Ripper, I'll have a hard time getting any information about Flora.
I'll try to steer the topic my way.
What a terrible story! I heard he sent a nose to Scotland Yard!
A nose? No. I think it was a kidney.
Wasn't it a heart?
Oh, really? I was sure I heard some terrible story about a nose or a disfigured woman...

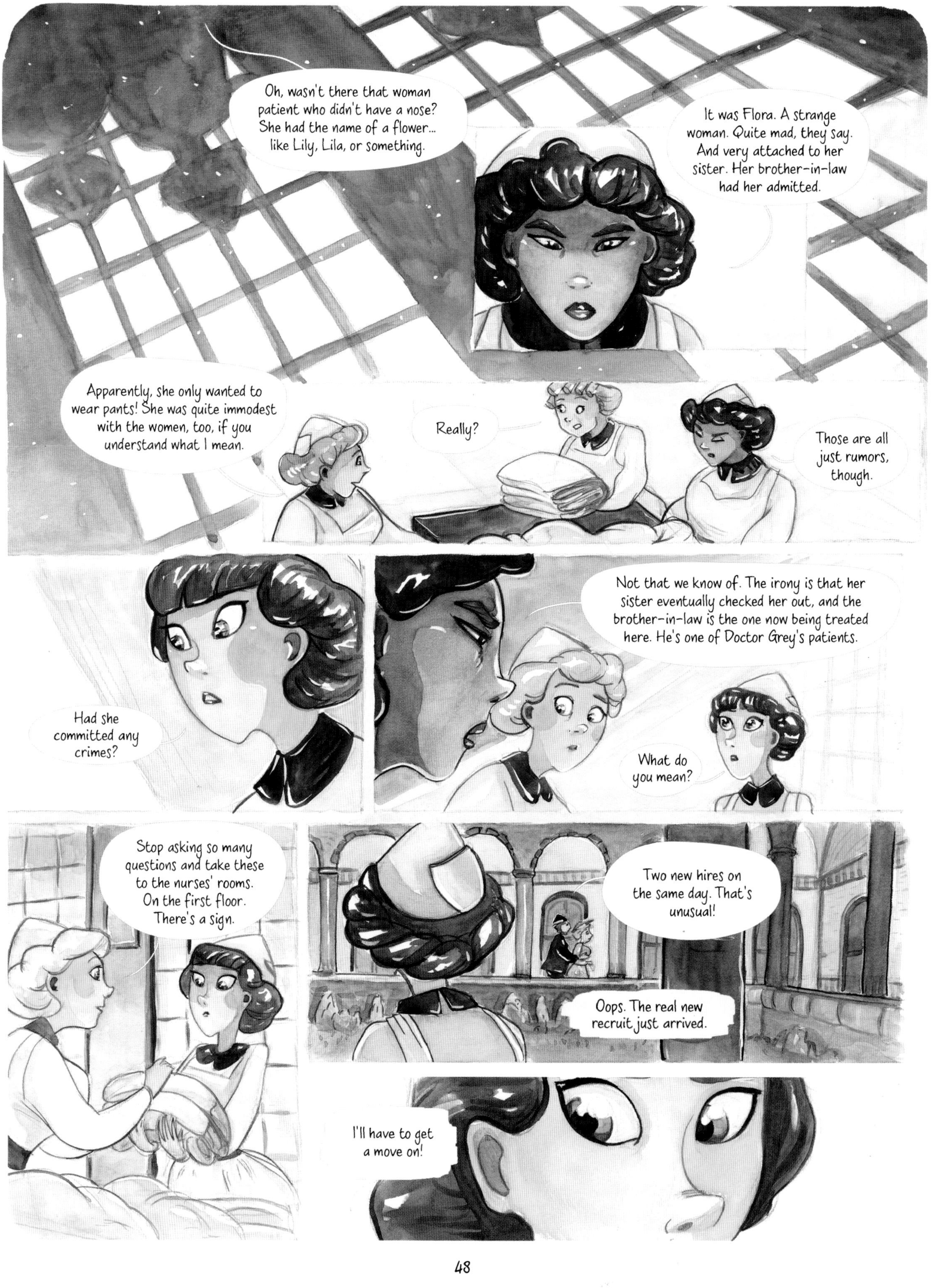
Oh, wasn't there that woman patient who didn't have a nose? She had the name of a flower... like Lily, Lila, or something.
It was Flora. A strange woman. Quite mad, they say. And very attached to her sister. Her brother-in-law had her admitted.
Apparently, she only wanted to wear pants! She was quite immodest with the women, too, if you understand what I mean.
Really?
Those are all just rumors, though.
Had she committed any crimes?
Not that we know of. The irony is that her sister eventually checked her out, and the brother-in-law is the one now being treated here. He's one of Doctor Grey's patients.
What do you mean?
Stop asking so many questions and take these to the nurses' rooms. On the first floor. There's a sign.
Two new hires on the same day. That's unusual!
Oops. The real new recruit just arrived.
I'll have to get a move on!

Flora's brother-in-law... in other words, the mysterious Mr. Kippersalt, is apparently a patient here.

Doctor Grey's ward: Department of Paranoid Men. I have a bad feeling about this. I need to make sure!

The doctor is asking for you in room 123.

Room 123? But I just gave him his shot!

Apparently, it wasn't enough. He won't calm down!

But I gave the right dose!

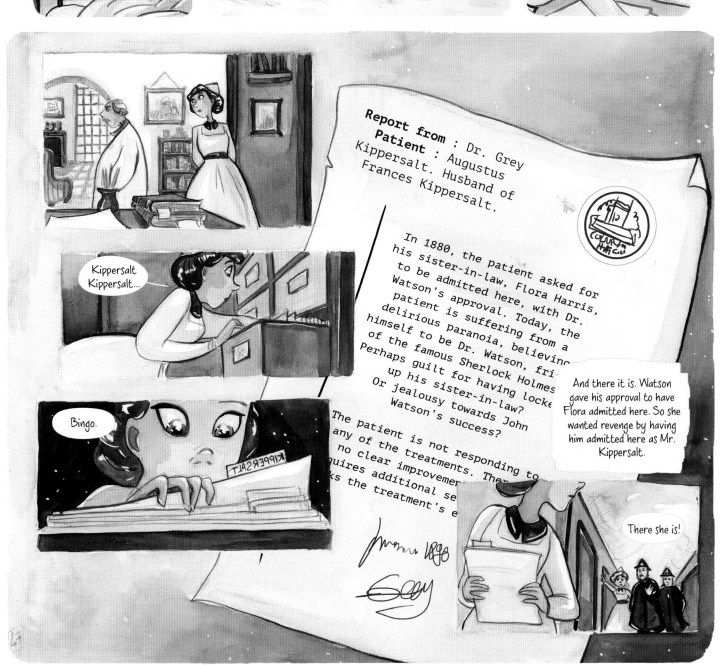

Kippersalt Kippersalt...

Bingo.

Report from : Dr. Grey
Patient : Augustus Kippersalt. Husband of Frances Kippersalt.

In 1880, the patient asked for his sister-in-law, Flora Harris, to be admitted here, with Dr. Watson's approval. Today, the patient is suffering from a delirious paranoia, believing himself to be Dr. Watson, fri... of the famous Sherlock Holmes Perhaps guilt for having locke... up his sister-in-law? Or jealousy towards John Watson's success?

The patient is not responding to any of the treatments. The... no clear improvemen... ...quires additional se... ...ks the treatment's e...

And there it is. Watson gave his approval to have Flora admitted here. So she wanted revenge by having him admitted here as Mr. Kippersalt.

There she is!

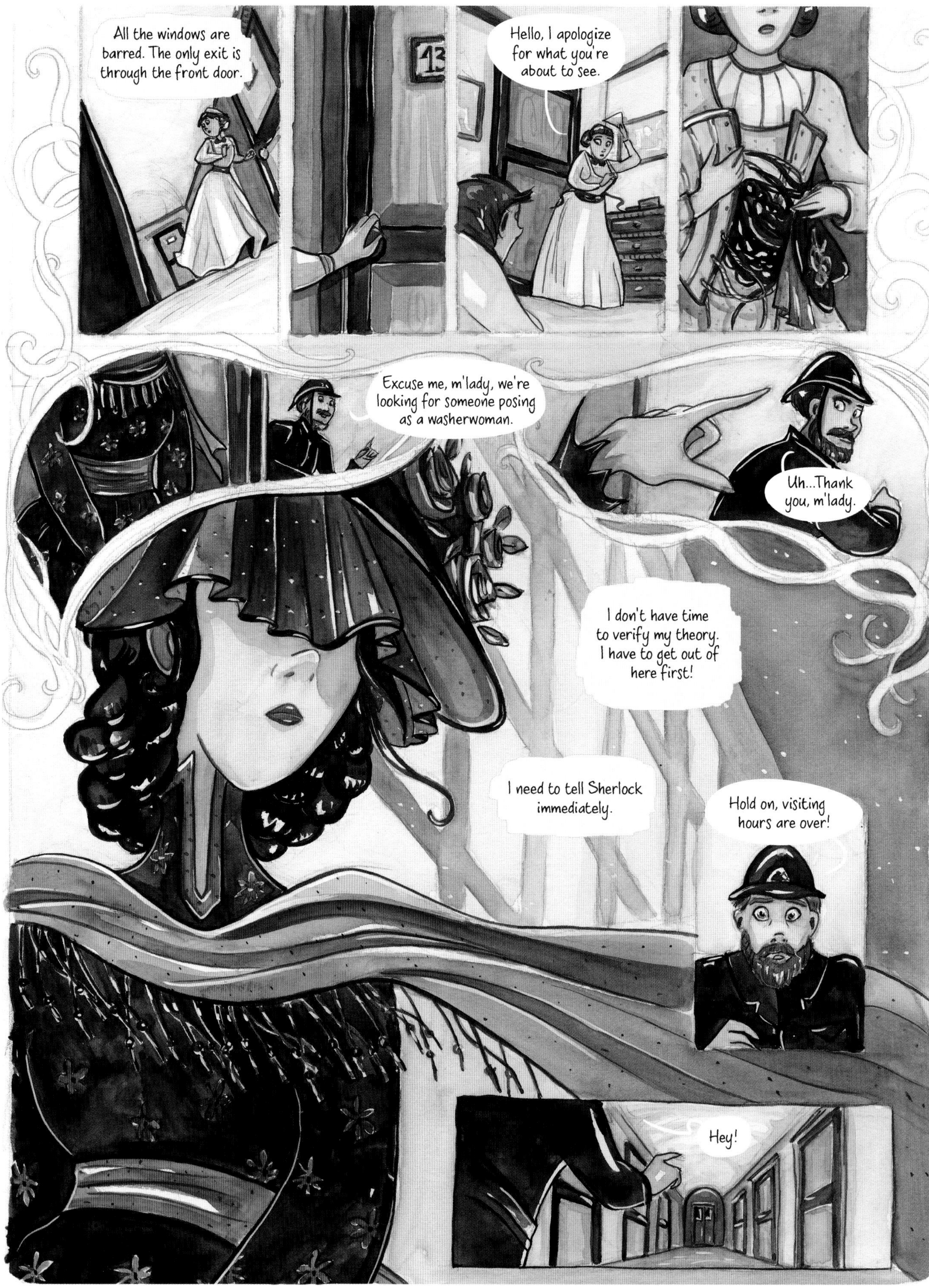
All the windows are barred. The only exit is through the front door.
Hello, I apologize for what you're about to see.
Excuse me, m'lady, we're looking for someone posing as a washerwoman.
Uh...Thank you, m'lady.
I don't have time to verify my theory. I have to get out of here first!
I need to tell Sherlock immediately.
Hold on, visiting hours are over!
Hey!

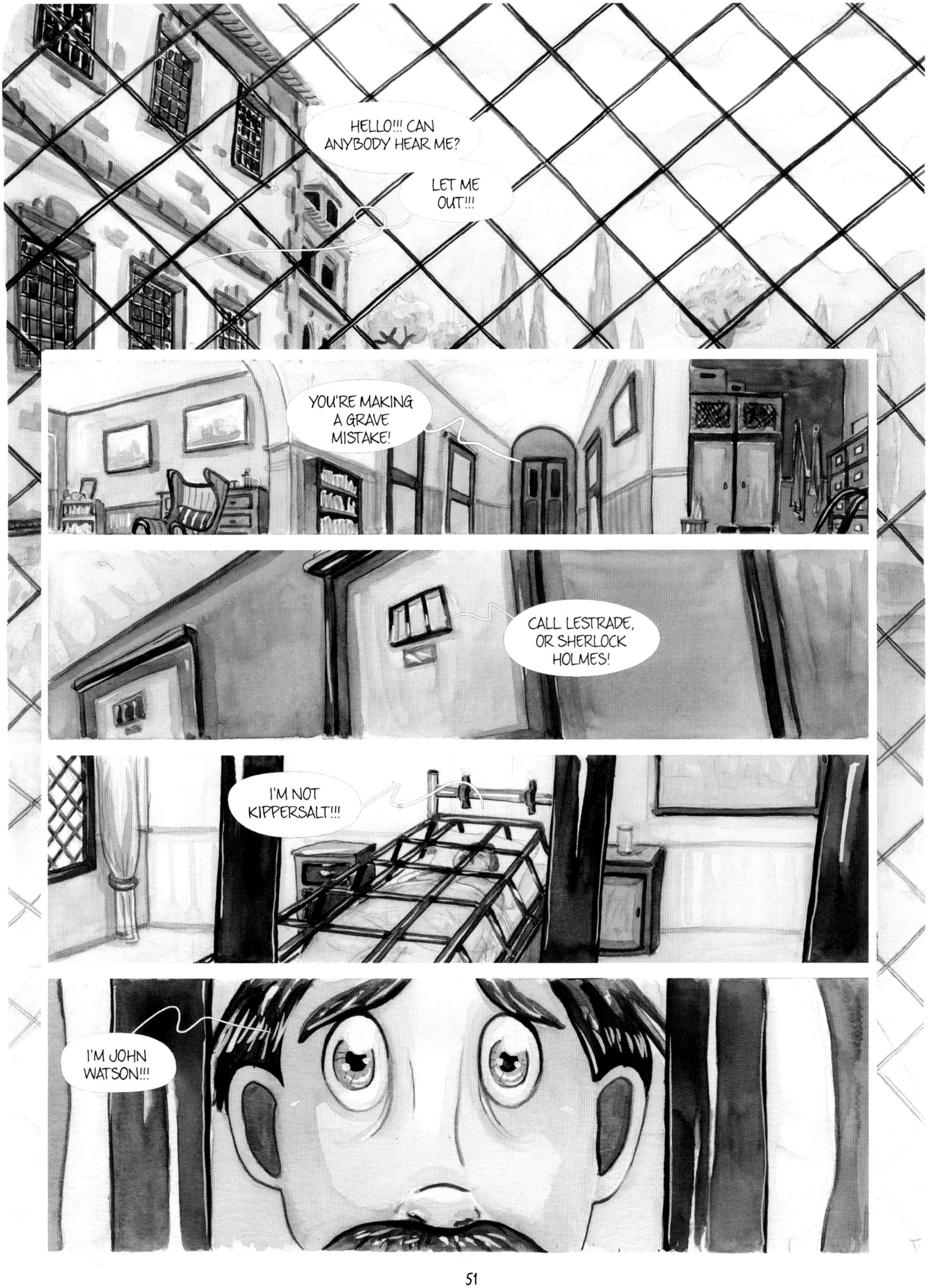
HELLO!!! CAN ANYBODY HEAR ME?
LET ME OUT!!!
YOU'RE MAKING A GRAVE MISTAKE!
CALL LESTRADE, OR SHERLOCK HOLMES!
I'M NOT KIPPERSALT!!!
I'M JOHN WATSON!!!

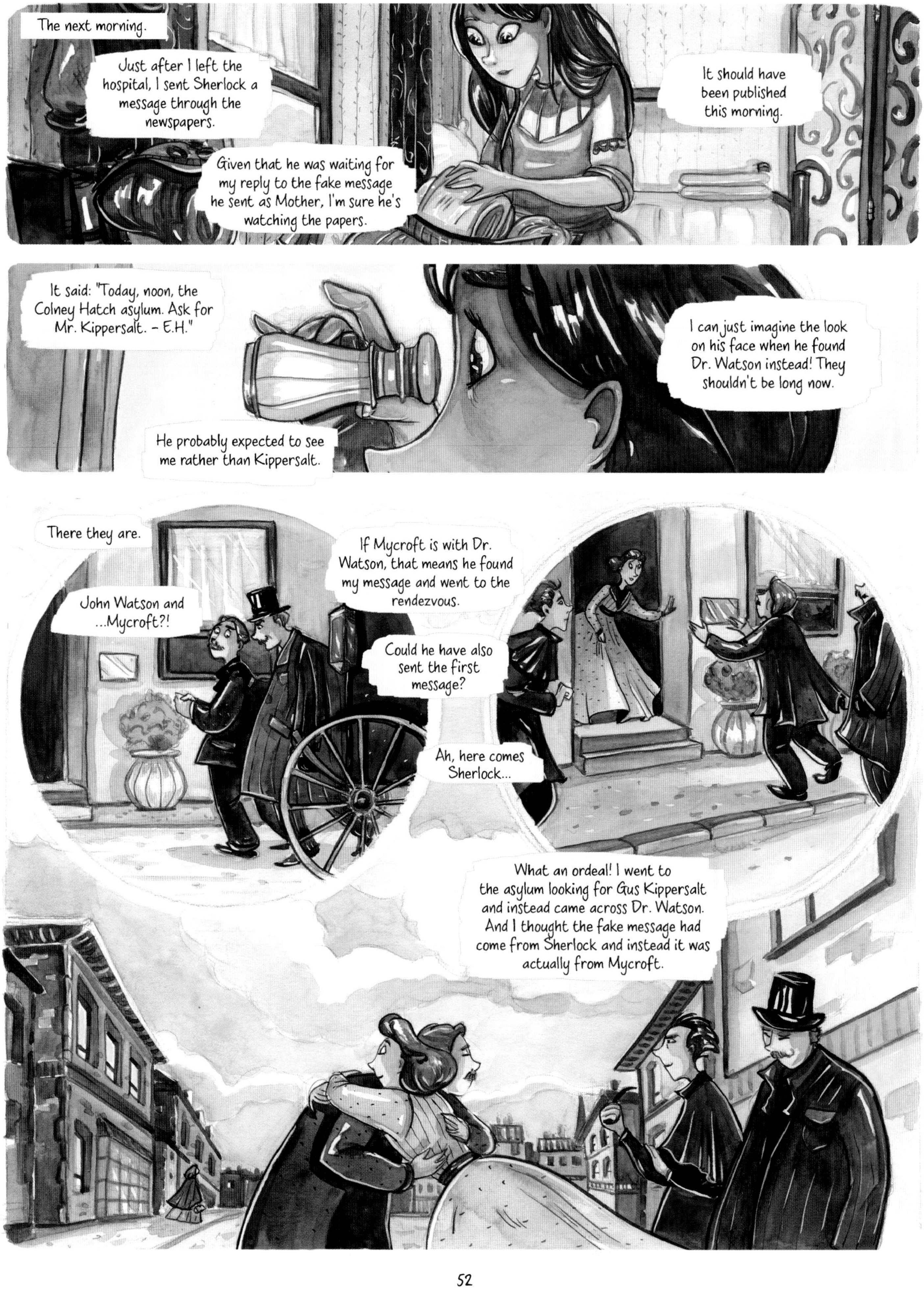

The next morning.
Just after I left the hospital, I sent Sherlock a message through the newspapers.
Given that he was waiting for my reply to the fake message he sent as Mother, I'm sure he's watching the papers.
It should have been published this morning.
It said: "Today, noon, the Colney Hatch asylum. Ask for Mr. Kippersalt. - E.H."
He probably expected to see me rather than Kippersalt.
I can just imagine the look on his face when he found Dr. Watson instead! They shouldn't be long now.
There they are.
John Watson and ...Mycroft?!
If Mycroft is with Dr. Watson, that means he found my message and went to the rendezvous.
Could he have also sent the first message?
Ah, here comes Sherlock...
What an ordeal! I went to the asylum looking for Gus Kippersalt and instead came across Dr. Watson. And I thought the fake message had come from Sherlock and instead it was actually from Mycroft.

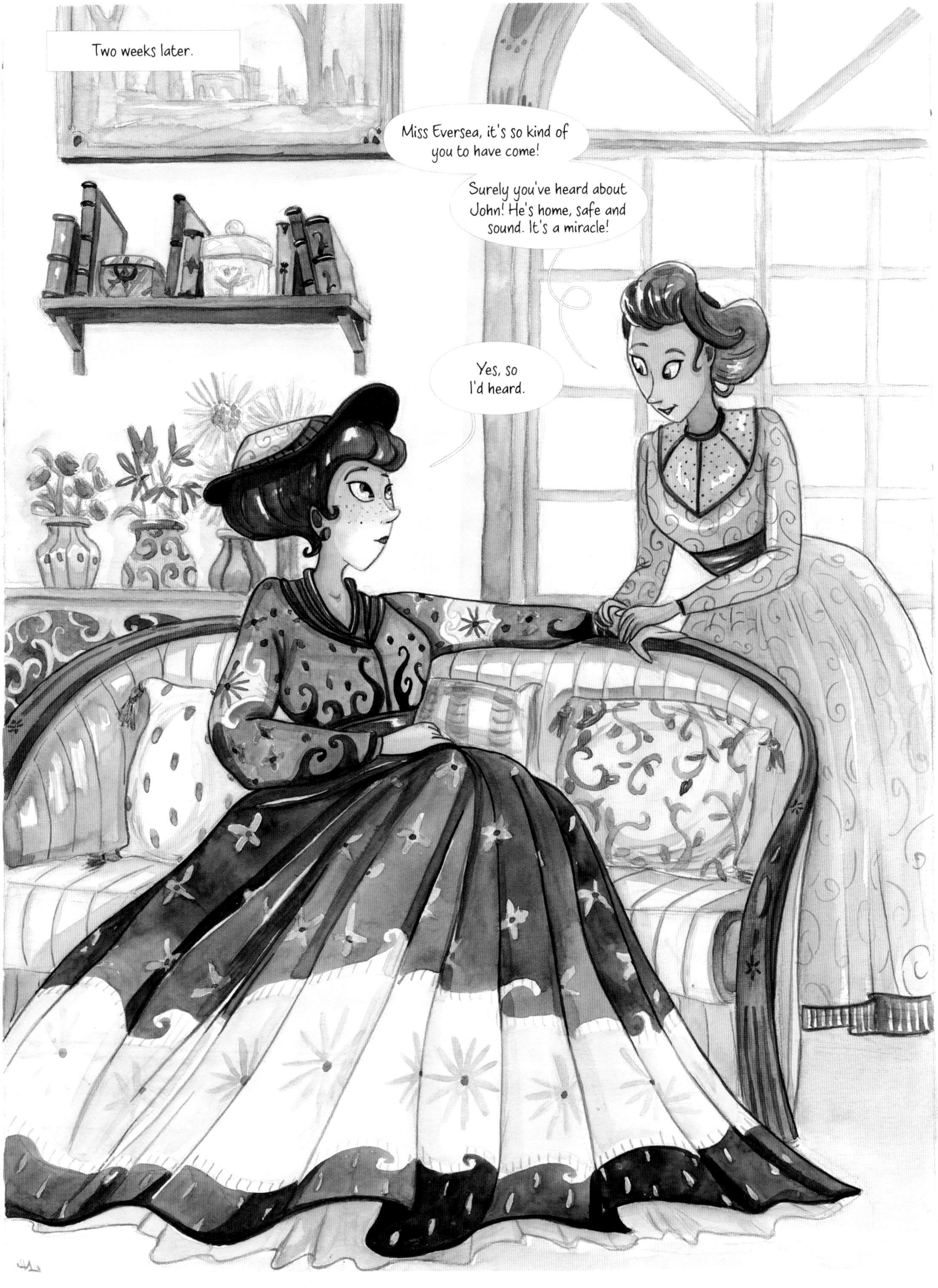
Two weeks later.
Miss Eversea, it's so kind of you to have come!
Surely you've heard about John! He's home, safe and sound. It's a miracle!
Yes, so I'd heard.

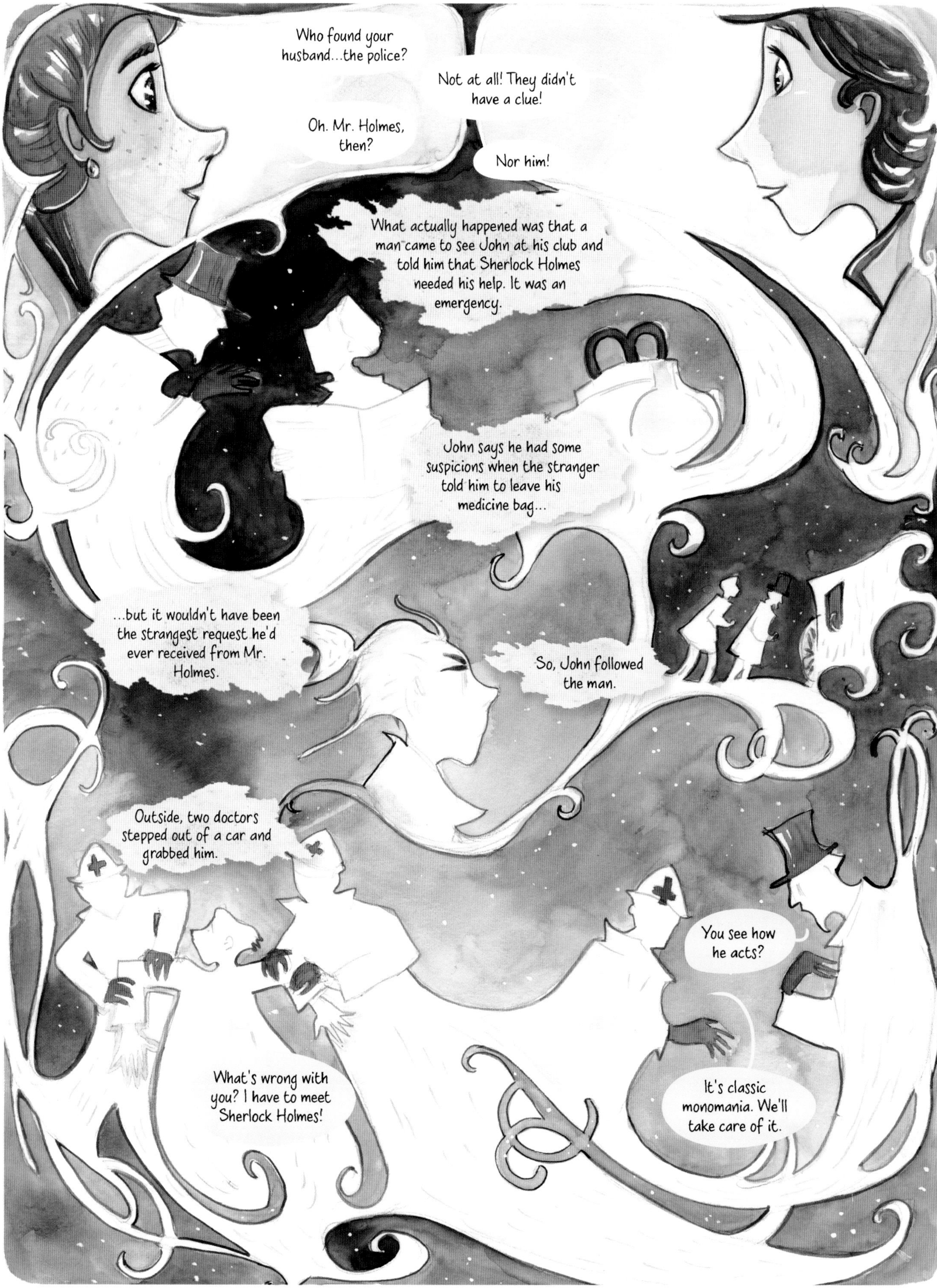
Who found your husband...the police?
Not at all! They didn't have a clue!
Oh. Mr. Holmes, then?
Nor him!
What actually happened was that a man came to see John at his club and told him that Sherlock Holmes needed his help. It was an emergency.
John says he had some suspicions when the stranger told him to leave his medicine bag...
...but it wouldn't have been the strangest request he'd ever received from Mr. Holmes.
So, John followed the man.
Outside, two doctors stepped out of a car and grabbed him.
You see how he acts?
What's wrong with you? I have to meet Sherlock Holmes!
It's classic monomania. We'll take care of it.

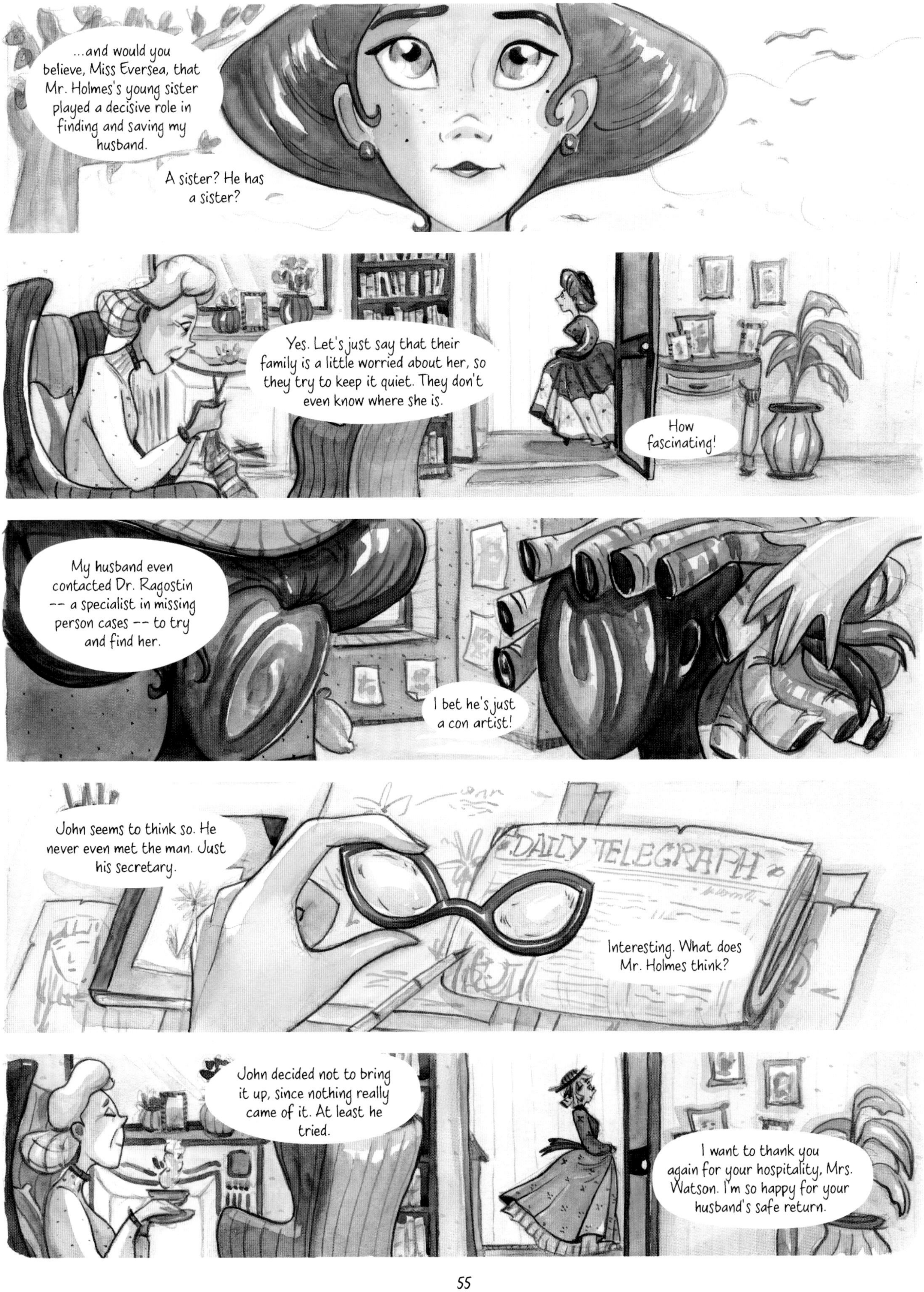
...and would you believe, Miss Eversea, that Mr. Holmes's young sister played a decisive role in finding and saving my husband.
A sister? He has a sister?
Yes. Let's just say that their family is a little worried about her, so they try to keep it quiet. They don't even know where she is.
How fascinating!
My husband even contacted Dr. Ragostin -- a specialist in missing person cases -- to try and find her.
I bet he's just a con artist!
John seems to think so. He never even met the man. Just his secretary.
DAILY TELEGRAPH
Interesting. What does Mr. Holmes think?
John decided not to bring it up, since nothing really came of it. At least he tried.
I want to thank you again for your hospitality, Mrs. Watson. I'm so happy for your husband's safe return.

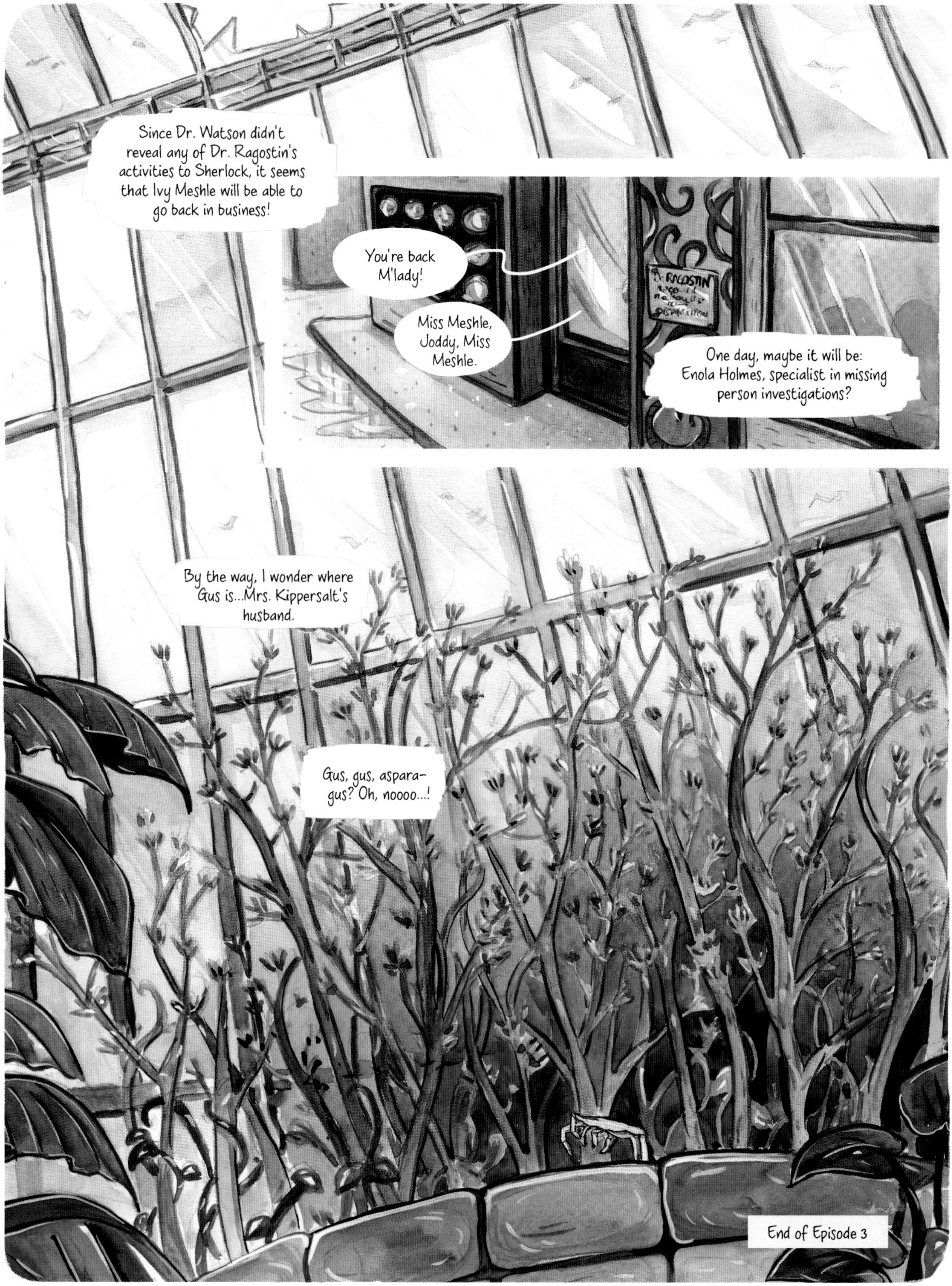
Since Dr. Watson didn't reveal any of Dr. Ragostin's activities to Sherlock, it seems that Ivy Meshle will be able to go back in business!
You're back M'lady!
Miss Meshle, Joddy, Miss Meshle.
One day, maybe it will be: Enola Holmes, specialist in missing person investigations?
By the way, I wonder where Gus is...Mrs. Kippersalt's husband.
Gus, gus, asparagus? Oh, noooo...!
End of Episode 3

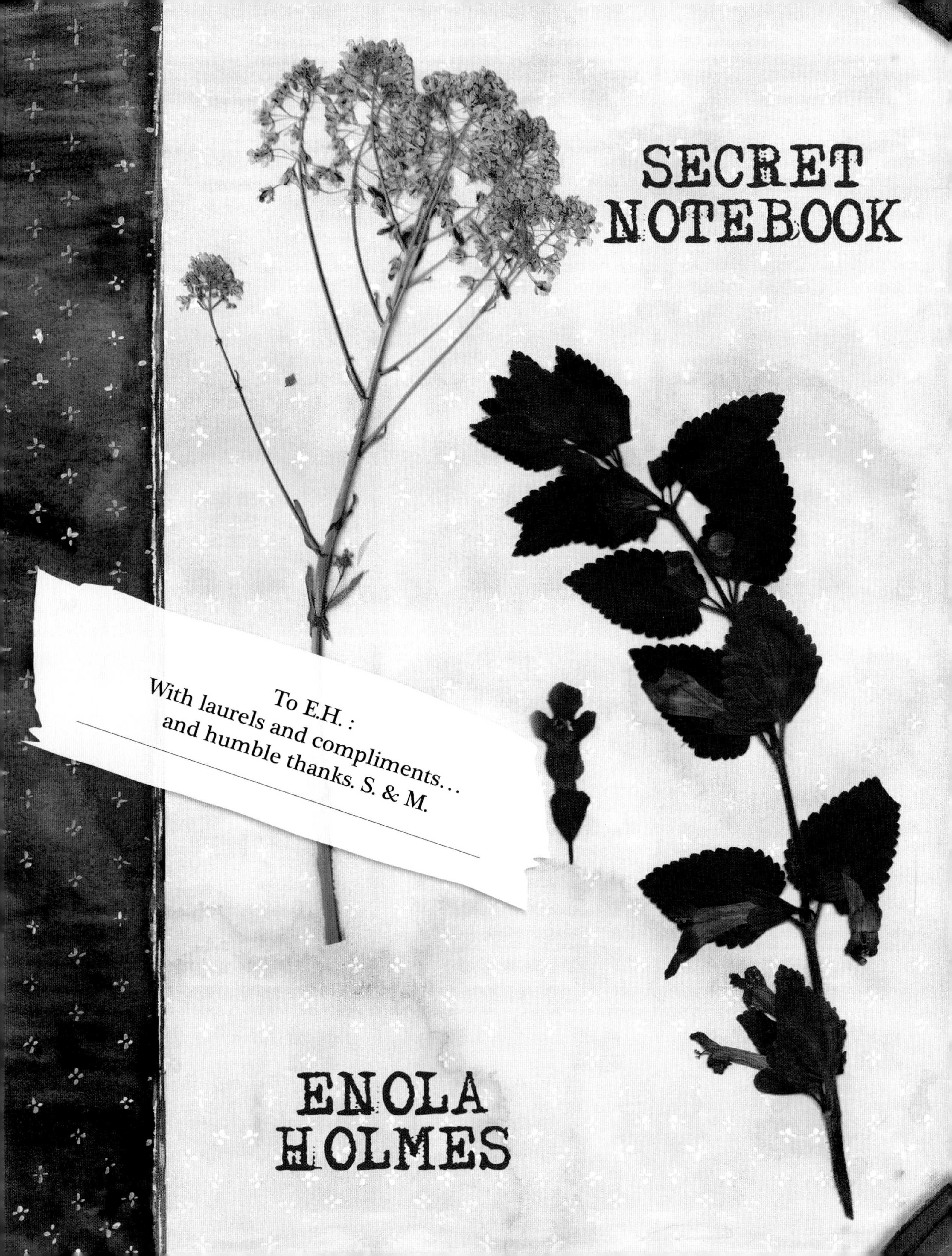
SECRET NOTEBOOK
To E.H. :
With laurels and compliments…
and humble thanks. S. & M.
ENOLA HOLMES

ERLOCK HOLMES ASSOCIATE MYSTERIOUSLY DISAPPEARS. DR. WATSON'S ~ WHEREABOUTS UNKNOWN

!!!

Alarming News:

The esteemed Dr. Watson, a friend and associate of the great detective Sherlock Holmes, has mysteriously disappeared without a clue. It may be possible that he has fallen into the hands of one of Sherlock Holmes's sworn enemies, as a way to exact revenge on the detective.

Another alarming theory is that he could have been taken by an anti-vaccination gang, for the sole reason of his work as a doctor.

An investigation is in process to retrace his steps.

Our thoughts are with his friends and family.

If you have information, contact us, or the police.

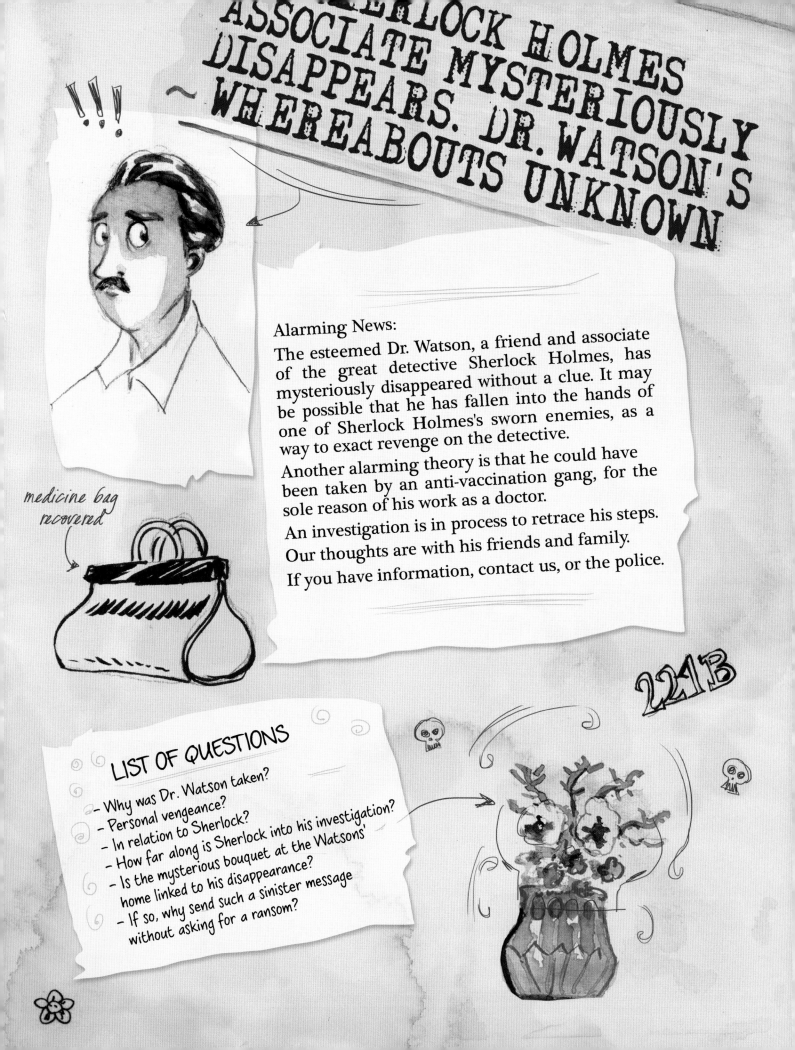

medicine bag recovered

221B

LIST OF QUESTIONS

- Why was Dr. Watson taken?
- Personal vengeance?
- In relation to Sherlock?
- How far along is Sherlock into his investigation?
- Is the mysterious bouquet at the Watsons' home linked to his disappearance?
- If so, why send such a sinister message without asking for a ransom?

422555 - 415144423451
22231142511523 5315
2415114341
111212513154155115445133
514354 5411

The message ~~Mo~~ther sent to the newspaper !!!

MYCROFT

(I) 1 2 3 4 5

ABCDE
FGHIJ
KLMNO
PQRST
UVWXYZ

(II) 1 2 3 4 5

25 55

First the letter, then the line.

Decode:

IVY, WANT GLADIOLA OR WHEN? AFFECTIONATELY YOUR CHRYSANTHEMUM.

ALOUETTE ALOUETTE
ETTUOLA ETTUOLA

Mirror message. Mother wanted to warn me about the fake message.

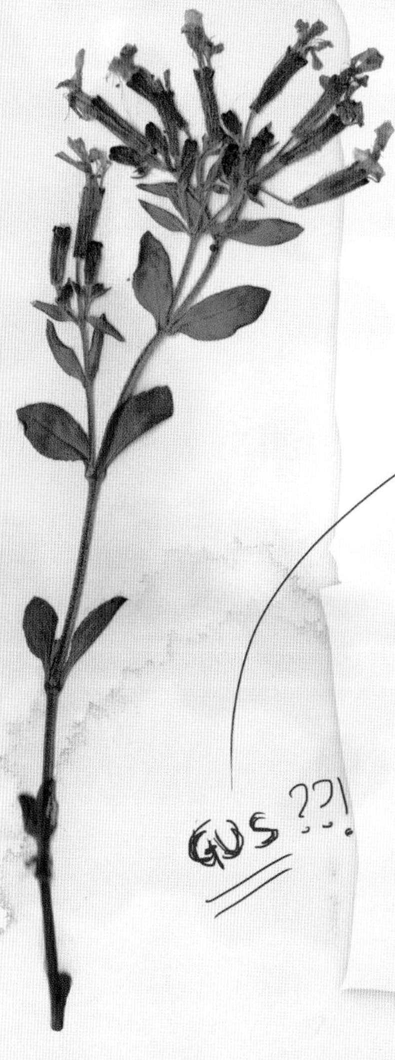

Using flowers for encoded messages

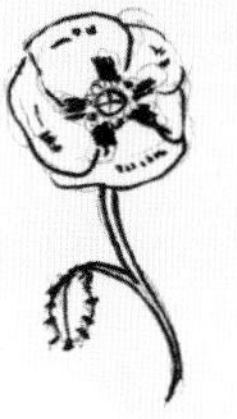

Red poppy : comfort.

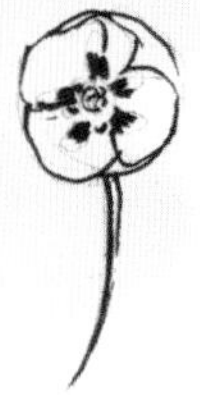

White poppy: sleep.

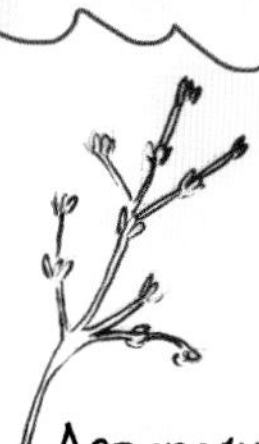

Asparagus: ???

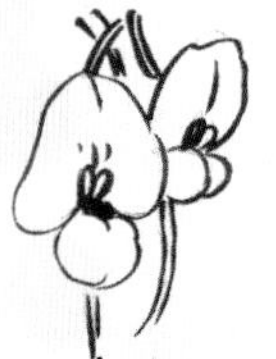

Laburnum: distress, abandon, dissimulation.

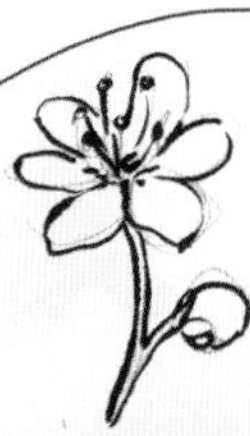

White hawthorn: hope.

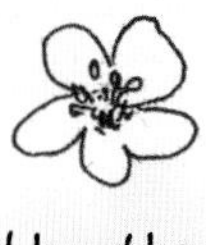

Red hawthorn: sorcery plant. Omen of bad luck in French culture.

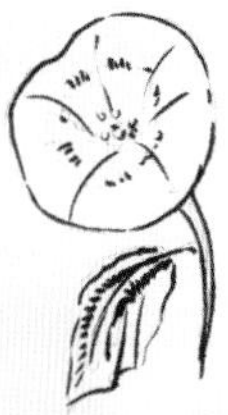

Hedge bindweed: invasive plant, lost hope.

GUS ??!

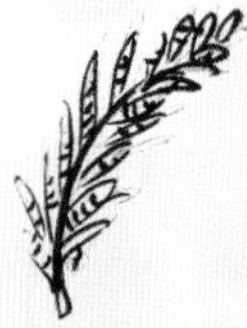

Cypress twig: mourning tree, grieving, bad omen.

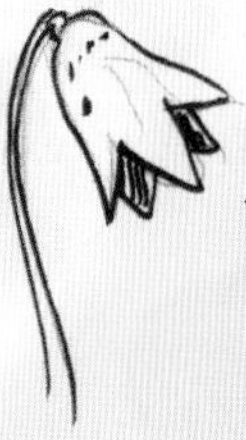

Bellflower: dejection.

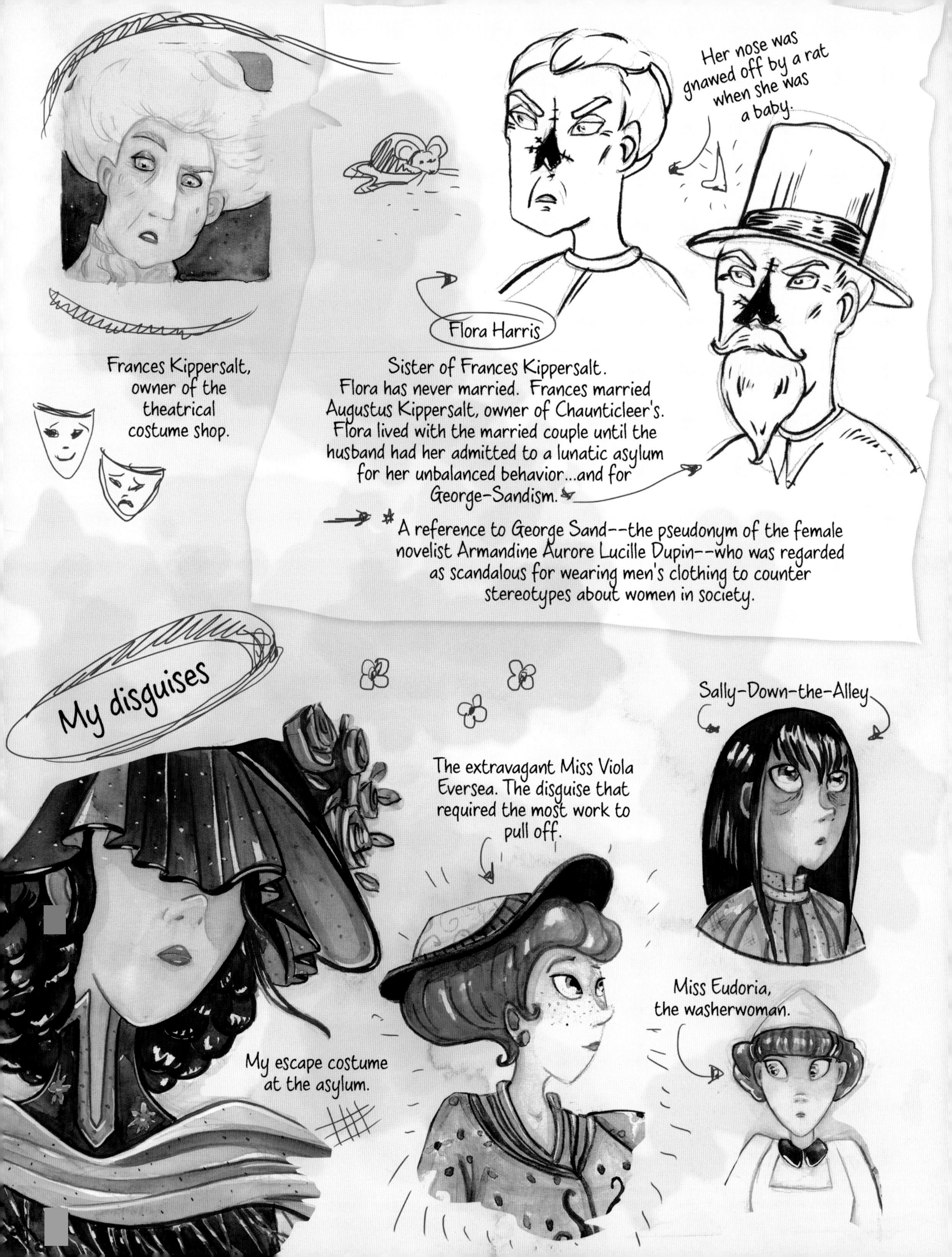

Her nose was gnawed off by a rat when she was a baby.
Flora Harris
Frances Kippersalt, owner of the theatrical costume shop.
Sister of Frances Kippersalt. Flora has never married. Frances married Augustus Kippersalt, owner of Chaunticleer's. Flora lived with the married couple until the husband had her admitted to a lunatic asylum for her unbalanced behavior...and for George-Sandism.*
* A reference to George Sand--the pseudonym of the female novelist Armandine Aurore Lucille Dupin--who was regarded as scandalous for wearing men's clothing to counter stereotypes about women in society.
My disguises
Sally-Down-the-Alley
The extravagant Miss Viola Eversea. The disguise that required the most work to pull off.
Miss Eudoria, the washerwoman.
My escape costume at the asylum.

221B

When I spent the night at Sherlock's lodgings, I searched his closets. He has many disguises. That's how I discovered the existence of Mrs. Kippersalt's store.

Fake mustaches, scars, and warts.

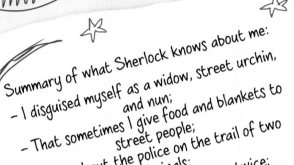

Summary of what Sherlock knows about me:

- I disguised myself as a widow, street urchin, and nun;
- That sometimes I give food and blankets to street people;
- That I put the police on the trail of two criminals;
- That I snuck into his home twice;
- That I use the name Ivy;
- So he might know that a woman by the name of Ivy Meshle works for Dr. Ragostin, especially if Dr. Watson mentioned it to him.

Several wigs, both men's and women's.

Make-up powder. And fake beards.

Not to mention the large number of his costumes.

The rooster sign.

PETERLOTE'S

Peterlote's store is a real gold mine. There were many fascinating trifles and oddities ...velvet roses, music boxes, feather fans, vizard masks, and much more.

Accoutrements to change your body shape.

ABCDEFGHIJKL
MNOPQRSTUV
WXYZ
YES
NO

Ouija board to speak to the dead, and crystal balls.

Perfume and make-up.

Wigs and masks.

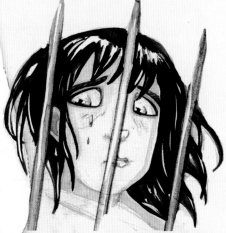

Colney Hatch

Colney Hatch Asylum - London - 1851

My time in the asylum was not a pleasant experience.

The lobotomy.

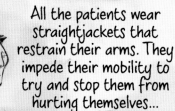

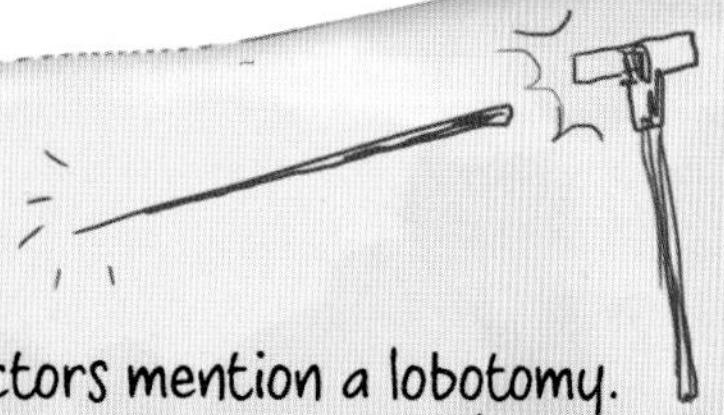

I heard one of the doctors mention a lobotomy. Mother finds that practice barbaric. It's an irreversible surgical procedure that accesses the brain through the eye. They insert a large needle, and then hit it with a small hammer in order to cut some of the brain's nerve fibers. It's used to treat mental illness, or migraines. After the operation, the patient becomes a total vegetable, incapable of doing anything on their own. Horrible.

All the patients wear straightjackets that restrain their arms. They impede their mobility to try and stop them from hurting themselves...

They all look sad.

Jack the Ripper

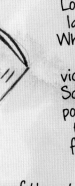

Serial killer who terrorized London and had many victims last year. He terrorized the Whitechapel district of London, choosing prostitutes as his victims. He sent their organs to Scotland Yard. According to the police, the killer could be part of the aristocracy, and would be familiar with medical practices. It makes me shiver.

The unfortunate victims :

1 Mary Ann Nichols
2 Annie Chapman
3 Elizabeth Stride
4 Catherine Eddowes
5 Mary Jane Kelly

One of the potential suspects is Aaron Kosminski, a barber who practices in the Whitechapel neighborhood. But the police lack proof and it's likely that the real killer is still at large.

The last word on the Kippersalt family.

BODY FOUND IN GREENHOUSE.

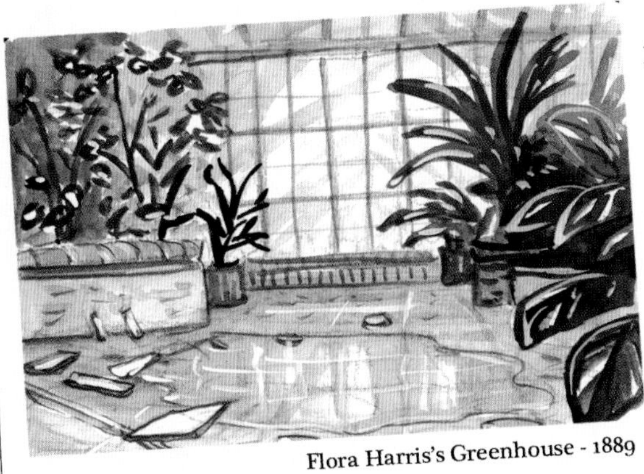

Flora Harris's Greenhouse - 1889

After Dr. Watson's rescue, the police began investigating Flora Harris and Frances Kippersalt, the people responsible for the kidnapping.

Overwhelming proof was found in the greenhouse located just behind the captor's building. After Sherlock Holmes carefully searched the premises, a body was found buried in a plot of asparagus.

After an interrogation led by Inspector Lestrade, Frances Kippersalt gave up her sister for the murder of her husband, Augustus Kippersalt. Flora then confessed to having committed the crime, the motive being that Mr. Kippersalt had her forcibly admitted into a psychiatric hospital. She also confessed to kidnapping Dr. Watson for having approved the admission.

So there it is. Flora killed Gus. Mrs. Kippersalt covered for her sister, and they hid the body in a plot of asparagus. The very same one that I fell into and that saved my life. A murder and a kidnapping, all for the sake of revenge.

Now, Flora will likely return to Colney Hatch and Mrs. Kippersalt will be sent to prison for conspiracy to commit the murder of her husband. A dark and sordid story, but at least it has a happy ending for Dr. Watson.

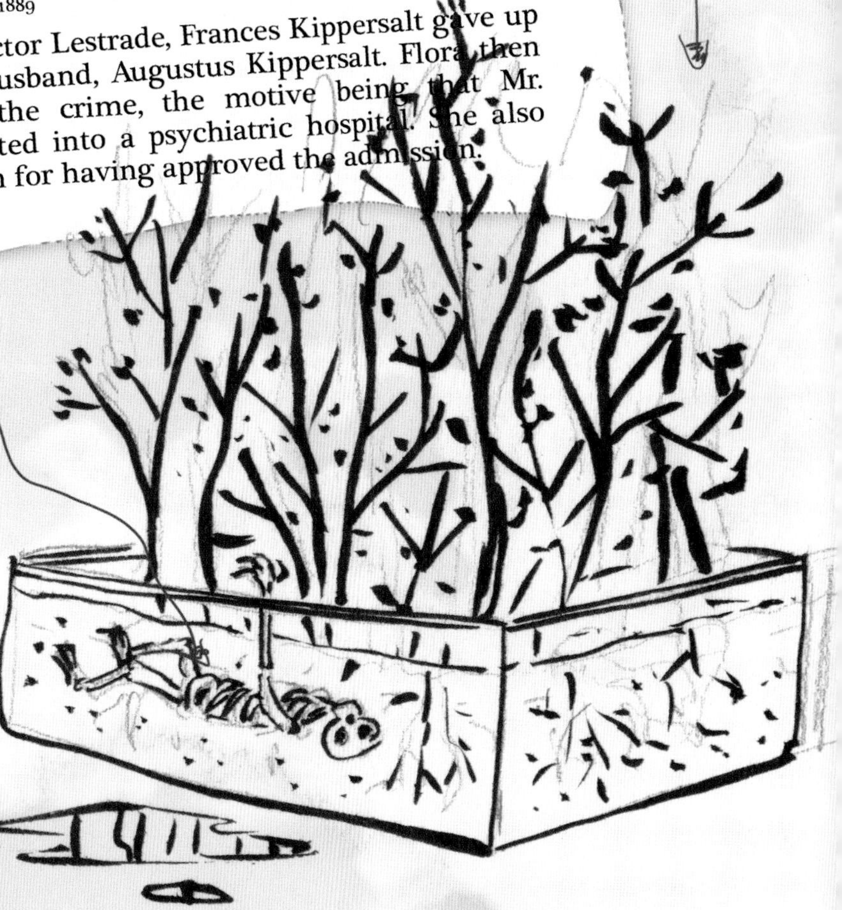

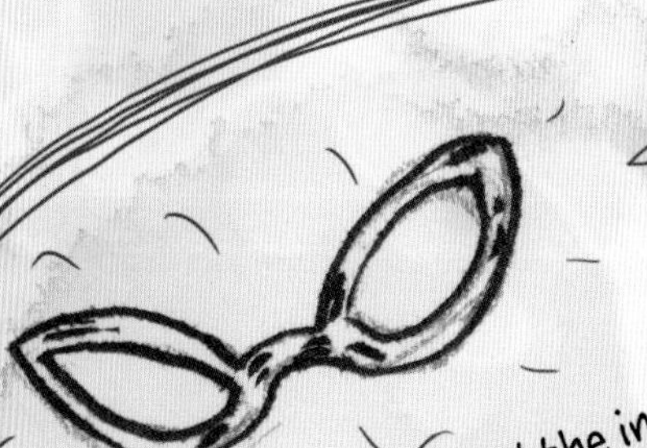

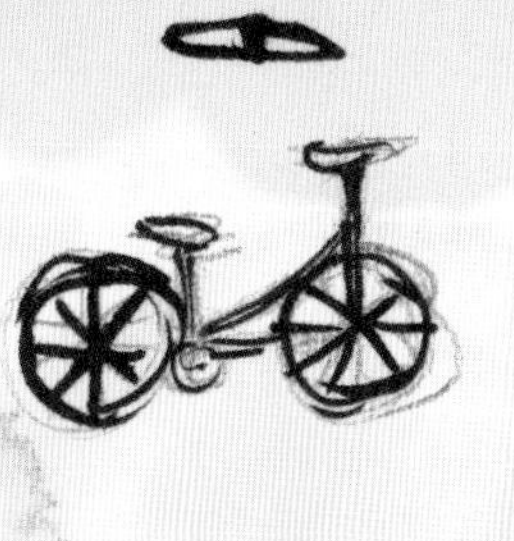

And the incredible good news is that Ivy Meshle can go back into business!